QUERENCIA SUMMER 2024

Querencia Press – Chicago Il

QUERENCIA PRESS
© Copyright 2024

All Rights Reserved

No reproduction, copy or transmission of this publication may be made without written permission.
No paragraph of this publication may be reproduced, copied, or transmitted save with the written permission of the author.

Any person who commits any unauthorized act in relation to this publication may be liable to criminal prosecution and civil claims for damages.

ISBN

978 1 963943 15 3
.
www.querenciapress.com

First Published in 2024

**Querencia Press, LLC
Chicago IL**

Printed & Bound in the United States of America

CONTENTS

POETRY 11

    Shed Cycle – Jessi Carman 12

    every bone is healed and every stitch is sewn – nat raum 14

    two rituals to reinvent yourself – nat raum 15

    The Cactus – Cat Speranzini 16

    Burn – Alexis David 17

    Herbarium of an Ocean – Alexis David 18

    Sizzling – Carolina Mata 19

    Cutting The Pain From My Body – Carolina Mata 20

    God's Teeth – Kerith Collins 21

    Spectrum: Girlhood – Arani Acharjee 22

    To, String—From, Puppet – Arani Acharjee 24

    Dark Secret – Arani Acharjee 25

    Suspended in air – Arani Acharjee 27

    The Garage – Devon Neal 29

    Imagine – Devon Neal 30

    Cathexis – Nikoletta Nousiopoulos 31

    glory thy glory appear unto thy children thy glory - Nikoletta Nousiopoulos 33

    mother ghazal - Nikoletta Nousiopoulos 35

    My Father is Liquid - Nikoletta Nousiopoulos 36

    Heatwave – Christian Ward 37

    The £1 M & S daffodils – Christian Ward 38

    The Underworld – Nico Vickers 39

    Very Hungry People - Nico Vickers 40

Museum of the Imagination – Robert Castagna 42

UNTITLED – Lana Valdez 43

UNTITLED - Lana Valdez 44

Asterisk Dust – Émilie Galindo 45

An Armchair Prompt & Black Page Navigation – Émilie Galindo 46

Fall Flips those 90s & 70s Sequins – Émilie Galindo 48

Excavating the Homesick's Blues – Émilie Galindo 49

relative normal – Maeva Wunn 50

renascence – a.d. 51

Skins and Shadows – Sam Woods 52

master of missing last week – Michaela Litwin 54

I break it down into two cars. I break down. – Michaela Litwin 55

Ambulance as Act II – Michaela Litwin 56

Ice Cream Truck as Act I – Michaela Litwin 57

Expired Produce – Michaela Litwin 58

The Storm – Abu Ibrahim 59

Ripples – David M. Alper 60

Green Reverie – David M. Alper 61

Glimpses – David M. Alper 62

Dark Victory – Allison Whittenberg 63

We know, Elsa – Allison Whittenberg 64

Sopa De Letras – Zaira Gomez 65

HEARD – Zaira Gomez 66

The Memories My Eyebrows Hold – Aysha Siddiqui 67

In My Mind Today – CLS Sandoval 68

I'm afraid I have involved myself into something I'm not ready for – Yuyi Chen 69

One for breakup - Yuyi Chen...71

Fourth of July, Another Day – Mark Kangas...73

Must There Be Valleys – Mark Kangas..74

I Never Hear Mention of the Caregiver – Mark Kangas 75

We Don't Speak of That Sinking Feeling – Mark Kangas.............76

Voted the Best Spot for a Coffee and Joint in the Keweenaw – Mark Kangas 77

Side-tracked - Claire Winter..78

Diamond - Claire Winter...79

My Own Personal Pompeii – Jack Anthony 80

Do the Damn Dishes – Liz Bajjalieh 81

A message for the modern-day colonizers – Liz Bajjalieh...........84

Emergency Am I – Audrey Zee Whitesides...86

Undercover at the Merch Table – Audrey Zee Whitesides 87

Mirror Multiverse – Marcella Cavallo 88

Indifference – Daniel Schulz 89

Untitled – Rachel Chitofu 90

FICTION 93

Sigourney Weaver Comes to Movie Night at our Duplex – Liam Strong 94

Additional Supernatural Discoveries of the Dog Meadow Light, Circa 2022 – Liam Strong...97

Bugs – Abhishek Udaykumar 101

Buses – Abhishek Udaykumar.. 106

Pink Vanity – Toshiya Kamei 114

Lake Melliza – Daniel Deisinger... 120

If the Holy Grail Were a Person – Eliza Scudder........................... 122

Move Right Through – Rebecca (Becks) Carlyle 131

Bluebells – Rebecca (Becks) Carlyle 138

Fosrsythia – Justine Witkowski.. 144

Wild Daughter – Jordan Nishkian 158

He's Right Behind You – Kevin B.. 166

Neonatal Cyborg – Elena Sirett.. 172

Synaptic – Christian Barragan... 175

The Thief of Bayfalls – Sebastian Vice 179

NON FICTION 187

Cigarette Clouds – Annie Williams..................................... 188

Practicing Nature - Lara Konrad... 192

We All Live in a Pokémon World - Kashawn Taylor 207

About the Contributors... 214

POETRY

Shed Cycle – Jessi Carman (she/they)

A snake sheds its skin
As I handle rebuff,
In a cracking, peeling malaise
My heart at its most vile
Growing only because
I have no other choice.

The myths I run to
Reject my supplications
And a phantom fist
Squeezes tight in my chest
Tense ball wound up,
Ready to strike.

But my flesh and frame settle
Into a haze
Catatonic under the heaviness
Of discard.

I tell you
Cut my belly open
Like a frog pinned to a tray
And amputate everything
I hate about myself,
Sever sinew
Let blood in excited spurts.

I spent my earliest years
Rescuing fractures of myself
But my resolve weakens
By the weight of the sword
I drag behind me.

In knowing you
I am supplanted from my soul
In favor of a malady
So sweet I dread
The fever's break.

My disquiet unhinges feral
At your easy disinterest
But you do not practice
Ennui to wound me,
I wound myself
That I cannot occupy its place.

It is the coward
Who is listless
And in pursuit of safety
I have run myself through
In pursuit of hunger
I have eaten myself
In sticky chunks.

every bone is healed and every stitch is sewn – nat raum
(they/them)
—After "Lipstick Covered Magnet" by The Front Bottoms

but the body begs to be sutured still,
bloody gums and falling teeth. i inch
toes closer to the cliff's edge and wait
for gravity to take me, angle this bruised
body towards gaping maw of canyon
and pull with the force of my weight.
(it's not that i want to die, but solitude
has siphoned my sanity, raised intrusive
thoughts to their own colossal powers,
and now all i want besides skin on mine
is for a hand with pliers to pluck each
tooth from my crooked jaw, then topple
me over.) dazed, i land in a river. i sink
to my knees and brace for the next blow.

two rituals to reinvent yourself – nat raum (they/them)

1.

discover yourself in heavy mist.[1] traipse like a midnight sinner to the center of a fallow field and sit yourself down. sway to the cries of the storm brewing to the southwest. when civil twilight draws nearer, enjoy your last moments of new moon's shroud over your most derelict desires. in the daylight, all there will be to want is yourself back. embrace the numbness. sit with it.

2.

find yourself in glitter dust. screech upward at nothing in particular, at the peak of the vaulted ceiling that is the night splayed before you. paint yourself violet into the cosmos with a fan brush. in the morning's goldenrod glory, beg the sky for another three hours of darkness. as the water mill of days and memories turns, take note of the past, and take care not to repeat it.

First published by Moist Poetry Journal

---

[1] "in heavy mist, in glitter dust" is a lyric from the 2014 Glass Animals song "Pools"

The Cactus – Cat Speranzini (she/her)

The cactus was a gift from a jungle cat that smelled of warm vanilla sugar with eyes as wild as storm-ridden Caribbean seas and sharp nails that left half-moon crescents down my back.

I am not going to water the cactus. Not today, not fifteen days from now, not ever. I am not going to call the warm vanilla jungle cat.

I am going to curl up like hidden prey in the corner of this room and exit when the coast is clear. But then the kitten bats the cactus off the windowsill, and it flies from its pot and lands on the floor.

So I move from my hiding spot. I scoop it up and repot it, pricking my finger, and a drop of blood falls into the parched soil as I return it to the windowsill. Blood magic, I think.

The kitten meows from across the room. I look at her, then back to the bloody cactus, then at the half empty water bottle still sitting on the coffee table. I said I would not water the cactus.

I have never been very committed to anything.

Burn – Alexis David (she/her)

Last night—flame throwers stood in my street, holding long wires of fire in their gloved hands, holding little buns of love in their warm palms: I was a stranger to them.

It was my friend Cyd's house; she looks so fierce sometimes. When she swears, it makes me want to spit on the ground like I'm a cowgirl or something. Her white hair burns us all up. They call her the silver fox.

The night air smelled of kerosene and silence and the summer, now dead–crinkling in embers on the ground. No one spoke as they put the northern lights to music, translated the radio static into synthesized sound.

No one spoke except a woman from Georgia who called up to a man in a tree, "Is it scary?"

Is it scary to catch yourself being alive, not drunk, but awake with fire? And you know, it's a controlled burn—sometimes it makes the plants come back.

Sometimes I think I should burn memories, all that time with those men in those beds with all that PBR and Essex Pub. Those men with tar between their teeth, but their ankles looked so kind in bike shoes.

"Is it scary?" I ask myself.
Yeah, it is.
It's that fire in the back of my mouth that really lets me burn.

Herbarium of an Ocean – Alexis David (she/her)

I stepped into a sea bath of my own drowning, into
silence: an ocean of bleached coral and

please can you hold me like a woman being baptized?
Me and Vincent got drunk on the boat.
It felt good to be so scared and free.

I thought the men were looking for sharks,
but they were looking for something else.
Men can be so beautiful, but it's not talked about enough.

Consider their delicate brown fingers.
Consider the whiteness of their teeth.

I wanted to tell you that I loved you, but we had snorkels in our mouths.
I wanted it so much to come back to life, but it didn't. It wouldn't.
Maybe it never will.

Could I kiss it?

Sizzling – Carolina Mata (she/her)

My brain is sizzling from the day
The week. The year.
The last few years.

Cracked open, yolk dripping,
Then bubbling in the grease of time.
Because nothing's greasier than life.

But there's no water in sight,
So I drink it up,
straight from the pan

Hot and thick down the throat—
let it gag me to oblivion
and swallow it all.

Cuz they always beg me to swallow
If I refuse it on the face.

And wait until I'm alone to throw it up
On the kitchen floor.
Like any other half-digested chunk.

And when I'm done with life and brains
and the spit loaded sizzling of it all
Coming up

out my throat,
I wipe it up with a wet towel
Off the greasy tile floor
Before my cat can come along to lick it off.

Cutting The Pain From My Body – Carolina Mata (she/her)

My body is breaking down.
My toes are swollen, ankles brittle.
My feet are filled with fluid made of my childhood.

      That's alright.

I take an obsidian dagger
and cut open the bottom of my feet
two thin lines, criss crossed,
to bleed out the past that's been built up.

A hiss of pain. A hiss of shh shh shh.
I whisper in the voice of little past me who shushed in the dark, once:

"Wake up momma, it's just a bad dream. Shh shh shh."

      "But the devil was chasing me," she said.
      "But my sisters were trying to kill me," she said.
      "But the men were holding me down," she said.
          "But it wasn't a dream."

"Shh shh shh, go back to sleep."
We both sounded so young then.

But I am not little me anymore.
So I dig a hole in the yard now, and whisper into it;
let the past leak out from my feet.

I've never bled this much before.
And when I'm done,
My poor, soft body feels too tender to walk.

So I push my belly into the dirt
and I slither home instead.

God's Teeth – Kerith Collins (she/her)

They are hypnotizing
There is never enough
My mind is distracted
These words are like a song
Magnificent and simple and layered
Bombarded by the light
Of this striking woman
Supple in form
Arms open wide
Smiling, beckoning me in
Endlessly intoxicating
The warmth is my comfort
Racing heart
There is never enough
Not close enough
There is never enough
My heart is light and my face is dry
Pools of tears fill my eyes
Not close enough
My butterflies are bees now
Embracing them
I hear ringing
All I hear is the bumble before the black...

Spectrum: Girlhood – Arani Acharjee (she/her)

G i r l h o o d.
every little girl who has dodged the bullet—
it was a direct hit, Cariño.
you just don't know it yet.
my mirror is a family heirloom
passed on by my great grandma, 12 years old.
my mother & i call it the "nightmare portal"
and smash our red lipsticks on the broken glass.
red looks better, fragile. my mama has taught me.
red has been my favourite colour ever since.

a stranger & i,
curated playlists over some bruises and tampons
until 2 in the morning.
what are we?
"he with a S"
s for? suffering.
s for? scandalous. s for? scapegoat.

To everyone with a double X,
it's in your nature to bite off the tongue
and swallow it with tears for breakfast.
What do you want, baby girl?
a (teddy) bear or the gallows?
Tell me what you want.
A pretty purse to carry your severed head?
Gourmet lies served on a silver platter?
(Fair)ness cream?
you're so ugly by the way!

i'm just a girl!
just a girl!
just a girl!
just a girl!

and girls are cruelest to themselves.
we are all sick; slowly decaying;
spreading rhizomes of girlhood spectrum—
snapping shoots by our necks so no one knows.
i'm just a girl
and girls are taught to drown in their own venom.

To, String—From, Puppet – Arani Acharjee (she/her)

you & i, an urban legend
spread across the valley of folk town.
our tale of glory passed through the hall of shame—
manhandled in a dingy car trunk at 11pm,
four days a week.
i need invisible hands to feel my limbs
and you are as inanimate as my dreams.
last friday i got a husband
and he ate up every corner of my stage
when i spilled stuffing as my stitches came undone.
folk town snacked on the scandal for 3 days straight,
but no one saw the added inches hanging by your tail.

thread of manipulation
who controls you?
who lets you restrain me
in this free fall illusion??

you are like an invisible prison that lets me float but fly.
irony is, i'll outlast you & your next 16 kins in the dingy car trunk
until it's time to let go.
one might think i'd break free,
no strings attached.
but this myth has its anchor spiraled in the fingers of the
puppeteer. so perish now because death comes in many forms
but the form of love is surprising.
die here as i slowly sever your heartstrings;
before the legend breaks you apart from my dangling limbs....

Dark Secret – Arani Acharjee (she/her)

hey, tell me a secret, will you?
which one?
a dark one?
from the boxes under my bed?
from the boxes under your bed.
can you take it?
will you make it? until the end?
i can't say.   for sure.
promise me.   you'll stay.
if i drift away?   i take your hand.
break into pieces?   i gather 'em all.
reek of ashes?   i wash 'em in my tears.
what would you do with a punctured heart?
i'll bloom lotus right inside.
what of the bruises? that i painted on myself?
i'll draw maps for a wonderland.
i wanna choke my mirror to death.
i wanna stain my white sheets red.
i wanna scream at the top of my lungs.
i wanna grieve and mourn and punch.
and i don't care who calls me insane.
do you and anything you want
but stay my love.   Stay.
play with your nails and teeth
for one more day.   just one more day.
it does get grayer, less gray, then gray.
i read the script somewhere.
of everything you said.
my world is blue, not gray.
and i'm drowning every day.
i know, i heard you the first time
it's one body, two crimes.

your scars are still all mine.
you didn't do it.   did you?
i did, but didn't make it.
you are a loser.   a sore one.
i can teach you too, how to lose.
we lose either way.
sure, but this side just smells better.
our brain is a killer anyway.
on sundays, we can befriend her.
what about sunday?   birth-day?
will you stay?   i may.
promise?   just for one day.

Suspended in air – Arani Acharjee (she/her)

mother, i be cloud today for all i want
i want it. i want it. i want it.
soooo bad.
no earth would bring me down, watch it
i be wearing gravity, my favourite crown.
it's worth it! it's worth it! it's worth it!
onnnn my head i swear.

mother, i be balloon today if i need
i'm high! i'm high! i'm high!
hiiiigh on helium.
my dangling feet, suspended in air
i be soaring, to my castle in the sky.
i mean it. i mean it. i mean it.
untiiiil my bubble is burst.

mother, i be dandelion when i can
make a wish! make a wish! make a wish!
blowwww me like stolen kisses.
breeze on my face, i fall apart
i be tiny parachute, in ballerina style
and i twirl. and i twirl. and i twirl.
flyyyy my way to the last beat drop.

mother, i be feather if i may
be lighter. be lighter. be lighter.
aaaand lighter.
lose my wings in exile, i did that
i be floating on the wind, in free fall
and down. and down. and down.
doooown i go headfirst.

mother, i am bird you see
it hurts! it hurts! it hurts!
blueeee my sky out there.
clipped my wings, yes they did
i be rotting in my cage, let my dream rise
i feel it. i feel it. i feel it.
motherrrr i feel it all now.

The Garage – Devon Neal (he/him)

After he left, the two-car garage
closed and locked. She told me
not to go in there. In the sun-brittle
glass of the bay door, a tooth-shaped
hole, where I'd peek, as long as she
wasn't looking, to see spiders settling
on the pegboard wall, centipedes gliding
across oil-speckled floor, hardbacked
beetles waddling across the work bench,
flies like beauty marks on the door.
She told me a snake slept cold
between the chunks of firewood in the corner.
In there, they only heard the wet munch
of basketball on gravel, the occasional
clatter of a missed shot.
I wondered if anything still smelled like him,
if any beard dust gathered in the floor,
or if a wrench, forgotten in a drawer,
held the black maze of an oiled fingerprint.
When nature takes over slowly—
mice pawing into insulation, a squirrel
paintbrushing from out of the rain—
how long until the old traces dust away,
how long until the walls forget?

Imagine – Devon Neal (he/him)

The kids have hijacked the word
to ridicule, to exclude:

Imagine being eight years old.
Imagine strawberry is your favorite ice cream.
Imagine thinking you're swinging high on the swing.

They come to me to resolve the conflict,
but I'm busy in April sun,
pink smears across my lips,
my toes tangling in the clouds,
imagining.

Cathexis – Nikoletta Nousiopoulos (she/her)

Cradled and guarded, I brought the baby
here. We journeyed.

The spit from the barn animals' jaws
needed to be blocked. The baby's skin

was too new. The interior smell was fetid.
Raw, the magenta of the cow's throat

held a doorway to a feral emergence.
Time for recompense, for sin of undoing.

Clouds evaporate the baby's delirious cry.
Like a prayer, the donkey grants hope.

Enraptured, in the shape of
surrender, I hammer nail into pine,

cypress, or cedar. Disaster.
Metal rush, abbreviate my breath,

so if angels overshadow, I tuck my faith
in the hay of mangers, and beg it not to

glow. These witnesses cannot lick or
dribble for the meat. The baby

must grow. The baby always grows.
This golden fog around us (so enclosed).

I'm the mother who was promised
one to bleed out and let bleed.

I can't repent
the part of me you need.

Barn full of flies. Book full of lies.
The last neck of an apocalypse.

Here, no one is nailed or beaten
or put to bed.

The baby fell off
the earth. God is testing you. God is

testing me. A heaven
we shot down blooms.

One day I'll be gone. I did the best
I could. I kept you warm.

glory thy glory appear unto thy children thy glory – Nikoletta Nousiopoulos (she/her)

When the planets
were pinned up
like blue hearts
above my life, the angels

beat their urgent fists
on the bolted door
of the Lord.
All my bones recall

those unnerved knocks.
When the end nears,
I anticipate rapturous blasts,
hard like the sunshined

day of my death. What else
should startle my children
from sleep?
I teach each of them

how to hide under the
hat of a shadow.
I don't mean
to linger, so we say

goodnight. I hold
their hands, as if their fingers
are branches ready
to break off the source.

I'm not the distance
between angels
and mornings when

we watch grass wave

through the glass
windows of our house;
Sudden thunder tones.
We look up; our mouths

open. Blue night drops,
globes wet
on the flats of our hair.
Do not be confused

of powders of moons,
your desperate mothers.
*I've them buried in
an abode*, said the Lord.

We forget to live by
the flesh of earth. We forget
each planet is arranged
and articulated. Unsure

if angels defend my
accusations, I scrawl my
greedy wishes in a tomb,
fold my children

into their beds;
there's nothing left
to fear besides everything
I am afraid of.

mother ghazal - Nikoletta Nousiopoulos (she/her)

under the lamp: wet dirt & dead dew. i taste your fetal blood
    smother.
earth was born to sanctify and hail; oh, Sarah of barrenness, oh,
    mother—

i discover a delicate body edging off the cliff of an ovary. i anoint.
if one bloodies an embryo in fear, then search forever for the
    abducted mother.

thus, under the dream rug, i cloak setting stars in a moon-spell
    glow.
a sunflower, full of seeds, bursts insects; birth is not pretty. New
    mother:

baby's paw in her mouth; the claw of a blade on the gum, on the
    tongue.
calling all children: billions of little fingers & blinkings, billions of
    mothers

clutch their bellies for a kick. i pray to a cockroach with a thickened,
    Abraham shell;
the warmth of my baby's wing is milk white. drink froth from the
    tip of a mother.

daughter smells like violets under an amniotic tank. she gulps the
    golden fluid down.
firstborn sons choke: to be childless again: to bear the curse of
    absence: to be a mother.

My Father is Liquid - Nikoletta Nousiopoulos (she/her)

Not by stone but by cancer, my father was afflicted.
Externally sturdy like a crab, but inside he turned blue.
He fled to the valley. He fled to the field. He is liquid.

St. Stephan, the deacon, not listened to or acquitted,
became a pile of Holy Spirit and haloes and Hallelu-
jiahs! Not by stone but by cancer, my father was afflicted.

And therefore, I've turned to Acts, I've become addicted
to searching for clues, it's true, I lost my eyes for you.
You fled to the valley. You fled to the field. You are liquid.

The Bible was not clear with answer. It never once predicted
I'd lose my father to encounter veins he'd break through.
Not by stone but by cancer, my father was afflicted.

Was I a bad child? Had the saints chosen me wicked?
I broke the written laws, I hurt my own father, it is true. I flee to the
valley. I flee to the field. He is liquid.

Lymph nodes sick enough to travel to lungs, I insisted to
God, let this be a mistake, this diagnosis untrue.
Not by stone but by cancer, my father was afflicted.
He fled to the valley. He fled to the field. He is liquid.

Heatwave – Christian Ward (he/him)

The heat turns everything canine:
Watch the thermometer ripen
like a tomato as we growl
over bags of ice and the last tub
of vanilla ice-cream in the store.
We flash incisors sharp like house
keys over the last of our finds
while jealousy expands its territory.
The lido and swimming pool
sometimes aren't enough to shake off
suits of excess sweat: we need
to be still like a gecko to avoid insomnia
biting us on the scruffs of our necks
as we struggle with basic commands,
watch desire tug on other leads.

The £1 M & S daffodils – Christian Ward (he/him)

are dreaming of greater things:
Not to be discarded like old milk
cartons once they've wrinkled
like post-bath toes. Look how

they admire the tulip bouquets
wrapped in cellophane crêpes,
gaze at the prim carnations
lovingly displayed, and salute

the garrison of boxed orchids.
Of course, there's a smidgeon
of jealousy: expensive bouquets
with sunset-blushed roses, irises,

hydrangeas white like wedding
dresses, and violet stars of clematis
make some daffodils retreat
into the cloisters of their bulbs.

Others hiss with serpentine stamen.
How they dream of reincarnating
as a near-ageless bonsai, while the bin
beckons, reminding them of a life
as finite as matches.

The Underworld – Nico Vickers (she/her)

WHAT THE MORTALS KNOW:
Persephone has sex in hell
Before she is pried from her husband
Whose fingers leave bruises on her arms
That last well into May

She is passed from hand to hand
(like some rare artifact /
like some precious metal)

Into the anxious embrace of her mother
A reminder
She belongs only to others

WHAT THE GODS REFUSE TO TELL US:
Does she love him back?
Has her insomnia been acting up again?
Who does she resent more?
Where does it hurt? Where does it ache?
Will the longing ever end? Or is it eternal,
Like her cyclical life?
Would she spit out the seeds, bloody like teeth,
if she knew then what she knows now?

First published in The World's Faire

Very Hungry People - Nico Vickers (she/her)

1st take:

The knife doesn't go into the meat

Easily

Like it's supposed to

Slide in

2nd take:

We have sharpened the knife,

Maybe five or,

Six times

The knife goes in like glass

3rd take:

My plate is full of meat

It drips

The salt clings to my fingers

The hunger makes me ache

4th take:

We can see the bone

We bring the plate to the table

Before I sit down my hunger

Wins

5th take:

one plate five people none

of us are sitting we are all

crouched over the plate

hands salty and coated with fat

-

if the meat falls on the floor

we gather around it like

starved dogs and there is

something about my teeth

tearing fat from meat that

makes me wonder why

i don't use my canines

more often

First published in The World's Faire

Museum of the Imagination – Robert Castagna (he/him)

At the Museum of Poetic & Metaphoric Machinery
the mirror composed my likeness.

Sitting behind glass I found the moon was a vowel.
The bones of the globe held the world together.

I kneeled under its weight: clocks within clocks
dominating our lives. The compass

pointing north. Vials held out possibilities.
Galileo's telescope stared endlessly

at the ceiling. The scope's timeless reveries
seeing more than ourselves. Our eyes and ears

tiny installations through brass microscopes.
What a wonderful display of structures!

Our words and pictures measured in gears and dials.
The needle quivering when I rhymed.

UNTITLED – Lana Valdez (she/her)

I had a dream I helped hide the bodies, and then I changed my mind. My brother was the killer. He was so angry but still, his hands moved carefully, our twin fingers along soft teeth and widow's peaks, until he made a whole pile of them. They were there, under me the whole time; they were in the floorboards. I didn't hear them until I put on cartoons, and they began singing along.

UNTITLED - Lana Valdez (she/her)

There's something about
the sweat, how it locks
you in, hair like a wet,
wild dog.

An aching,
not hunger
but wanting
to be full, my
hot breaths,
writing
words on
your skin.

In a room full of ceramic gods and
guitars covered in white cloth,
you bare your teeth, your eyes
and my eyes, and

I know what to do with my hands.

You hold me by the jaw, prying
open, and you want to go deeper,
all red skin and raw lips, missing
teeth.

Asterisk Dust – Émilie Galindo (she/her)

INT - BAR – NIGHT

Early 90s synthesizer synthetic sound & a narrating asterisks & Light shafts with a hunch
What Is Love? *forms the anachronistic dust trail of the night. Like looking through 3D glasses. It's there, the denied depth. A question & a curse. Followed by an appeal disguised as a lover's plea—like some dressed up their religious fervor as love songs.*
Baby, don't hurt me. Don't hurt me, no more.

Wide shot of the dance floor followed by portrait shots of the pair. Picture them: 2 twenty-year-olds. Not so much dancing as wobbling. They haven't met yet. Their outlook on life is like 2 CDs on a turntable: overlapping.
20. Like dance music. Full of a heady sense of freedom in the rises. Exhilarating beats. & futuristic vibes.
Green & red beams scan the disco. Gliding & groping. Dizzy like a roulette wheel…Looking for something…
They meet. Strobe light slurred sight & whisky-wonkied eyes. Eardrums riding the buzz. For now.

So, 20 they don't know or recognise the dust trail of the asterisks that dashes through the night with the beams. The rummaging beams.
The next day's aspirin came with a question & a curse. The ringing in their ears soon turned into wrung arms by overbearing parents who'd lost their moral bearings. But here I am. Carrying her name proudly like a puppy from the pound

Background sound: muffled *What Is Love?* **& ear hangover buzz & an uneven aftermath fizzle**

An Armchair Prompt & Black Page Navigation – Émilie Galindo
(she/her)

INT - DARK LIVING ROOM - MULTIPLE ANGLES

Getting snagged on a dropped name & a shrinking sofa with an upholstered holster
Wide shot of a room, low angle, side view.
From left to right: a woman is slouching on a large & lay furniture sofa.
She is wearing paisley PJs.
Her legs connect the dots to the coffee table.
Empty, negative space between the table and the television.
On the ceiling, over the coffee table, a lightbulb is snoozing.
POV shot of the TV, slightly low angle:
A young man. A father. One knocks, the other shuts the door.
That name.
Counter shot, frontal, high angle:
She's jolted up. With her right-hand, she cups a stillborn scream.
Muffled ripping sound.
She brings her legs back onto the sofa. Folded against her belly.
The sofa—acing silent space holding—and its empty seat make her look little.
POV shot of the TV, soft—if not wet—focus:
Credits roll. Aretha Franklin's *Let It Be* preaches from the profane pulpit.
REMOTELY CONTROLLED DARKNESS FALLS
Ellipsis

INT - CORKED OFF CORTEX ON EYELID CANVA - OPEN CAN OF WORMS' EYE VIEW

Fabric softener backdrop & Frankensteined Meaning & Negated space
Sharpening focus, wide crab shot:
A framed line of green butterflies stenciled on a white, lumpy wall.
We slowly move to the left, following the green butterflies. Like bug crumbs.

Shadow letters are hanging, clothes: pinned to the green line under the butterflies.
To a full, back shot of a girlish woman sitting at walnut Davenport desk. Wearing her paisley PJs.
Cut to over the shoulder shot: looking down as she is composing a letter.
The addressee and some of the other words are blurred by condensation. As in you're so close to the window your breath keeps you from seeing.
A voice-over starts munching the letter's content. The name is spat out like a cleaned-out core.
We **zoom in** from above on the rectangular page. It becomes a door. As we **zoom out**, we move back behind her shoulder. **Full, hip level shot.**
She curls her right hand into fist. But it won't knock. Stopping millimeters away from the door. She tries with her left. Tries slapping the door. Tries tapping gently with her fingers. Tries kicking and kneeing it, but nothing gives.
Counter shot, closeup: She pulls the letter out of her hair and crumples it.
Counter shot from over her shoulder: scrunched-up letter is now a VHS cassette. It hisses away from the present.
Counter shot, closeup: She puts the cassette back in her hair. Her nose moves. She can smell the liminal lilac. She remembers she is in a negated space
Wide shot, eye-level: She is standing in the middle of a room. In her PJs. Behind her there are two sets of bulbous, late 80s TVs. On her right, a 70s brown, careworn, floral sofa. On the walls, posters of 80s classic films crowd the room.
Counter shot: double doors. Only one is open. The boy who had earlier knocked on the door is here. BOY
(sheepishly)
I think you could be my dad.

Fall Flips those 90s & 70s Sequins – Émilie Galindo (she/her)

Autumn / perfect sun
to milk or chocolate to wind
ratio in / amber
glass bowl / On the wall
tear-off calendar is purr
-posely running be
-hind / your name day / you
get to peel off / in-between
she knows / Time rushes
us / like Tetris theme
It feels good when things line up
bowl of chocolate stump

Excavating the Homesick's Blues – Émilie Galindo (she/her)

Paperback tongues have been flicking at the Foreign Four for a couple of days now. Some seem to be downright speaking in tongues. Ideological jargon.
Dig it?   Yeah, we get it.   No, roll up your sleeves. It's not getting.

From the frozen clock tower—both hands taking an endless drag on 4—they see a fenceless & gateless creedscape. Down to the wealth of tables—scattered across the place for spontaneous congregating—to the potluck amphitheatre or the trainless train tracks.

The tracks resemble a fallen ladder. Rungs of wildflowers & beads & pansies & ribbons & thyme & carnations & rosemary. The grown offerings highlight the tracks like a quote on a page. They haven't finished the book yet. They're reading its geography. Its iconography

They also visit a sanguine bus. A metal kitty—different feline, same spots—fossilizing in the grass. On its ribs, the visual of the bubble-gum mind of the frozen clock tower. Taxidermy. The seats are there, albeit gutted of their purpose. Rigor mortis. Revered.

*Excerpt from Acid Taste: Excavating the Homesick's Blues
(Querencia Press, 2024)

relative normal – Maeva Wunn (they/them)

five four three two one
will you make it home
if i don't count the
steps
one two three four five
will you stay alive
if i don't count my
breaths
i dropped a cup
and it hit my right foot
and left a terrible bruise
so i need to drop
another cup on
my left for
balance
chew one bite on the right
chew the next bite on the left
held my keys in my hand
while i put on my jacket
held my keys in my hand
to take it off again
we joke and say
i need things done
properly
but if they aren't
my brain decides
i need a needle
in my eye
and then today
i didn't tell you
to be careful
on the road
so now i'm sure
no matter what i count
you'll die

renascence – a.d. (she/her)

1.
you were half dead and no longer dreaming.
consulting with defunct gods, fragile-boned lovers
only caressable through white cottoned hands.
a fleeting emotion upon the ceaseless
eyes of Alexander, perpetually unfluttering.
she penetrated your coffin of dust and parchment—
a wild light, blazing.
you could see through her skin that her soul was ripe
for picking. witnessed only by eyes unseeing
you touched her throat and her words
were no longer empty.

2.
away from your scholarly prison, sheltered
from the marble eyes of the dead.
she takes you out of your skin, an idol trapped
in a clouded niche and breathes onto you
and her breath is butterfly wings.
she parts the curtains of her body and beckons the exiled sun—
this mausoleum is now flooded with light
and your heart
is no longer empty.

Skins and Shadows – Sam Woods (she/her)

I ask him
Does the moon move you?
And I can tell
he doesn't know how to answer.
His uncertainty orbits like a hesitant punchline.

And so
I try again.
*What I'm trying to ask is
how does your skin fit?*
Still,
I get nothing in return.

*Like a sweater?
Or a suit?*
I ask the question hoping for a shared understanding,
but I can tell—
he still doesn't understand.

I push on.
*Mine fits like a mat of worms—
they writhe in their own ecosystem.
Separate from me.*

I don't control it.

I can tell I'm making him uncomfortable now.
I want to back pedal
but I don't know how.

*The meat, that's what I control
but the skin is different...*

I trail off.

I consider my next move.
I think;

*If my skin is worms
and my insides are meat
then what is my heart made of?
I'm relatively certain
I don't control that either.
But who can be sure?*

I consider telling him;
*My brain is a globe
cracked at the hemisphere,
separating over time.
An unseen hand gives
it a spin on occasion,
but I never know
when it's coming next.
So, I oscillate on my axis.
In the gap between space and time.*

Instead of that, instead of any of that,
I shake the thoughts from my head.
I pick up my drink
I take a long sip,
and laugh at my own joke.

*The meat of control dangles
while the elusive skin plays trickster.*

A joke with
no punchline
but the dance of our thoughts.

master of missing last week – Michaela Litwin (she/her)

i'm chronically nostalgic
i've been carrying memories in my pocket
flinch when i feel them on my fingertips
so i put them down & sort em' out
two for you , three for me
i'll call you in a year
when i take them out to breathe

remember that spring

i sat by the dugout and watched you sink white leather
i began to cry
and blamed it on the weather
you laughed at me & asked if it was your swing
how do i tell you?

that this happens every may

in april i long for july
but the 4th comes along
and i'm hanging onto june
at the time i was missing another moment
that meant nothing to you
i wasn't lying when i said
sunshine makes me sleepy
and rain dries me out
it's the days that went by in silence
i remember being so loud
i am chronically nostalgic
now i've got holes in my pockets

I break it down into two cars. I break down. – Michaela Litwin
(she/her)

It's innocence
It's life
I hear an ambulance siren,
I say that's god's
How lucky

It's death
It's the end
but watch an ice cream truck drive by
sick joke
are you to be alive?

Ambulance as Act II – Michaela Litwin (she/her)

The cars clear for sirens and anxiety ensues
My pop would say 'you better be praying for whoever's being pulled'
Up until 7, i held my breath under bridges
Never believed in god but i needed someone to retreat in
I was 17 and smoked too much weed
Driving through my hometown & picking up speed
I cruised behind an ambulance for what felt like an hour
Convinced myself i was dead
A chariot of red leading me to a *much* holier-after.
I still hold my breath, but now it's only in my sleep
That's where i escape myself
For 6 hours i can breathe
See the lights flashing, and pull aside
Let them go past,
In my sleep, In my escape, in my fear

i too, i died

Ice Cream Truck as Act I – Michaela Litwin (she/her)

the kids are burning rubber on molten top
all to chase icy's and sticky-pop
i wait for you to tell me it's a cheap life
and tokens are paid with time that has gone
i wait for you at the end of the driveway
to tell me i've spent the currency all wrong
i look to the big kids on bikes who fly down the street
i think you all have the secret as to how you breathe so free
your lungs don't collect dust but you always choke on your words
i look to you for meaning
i kneel to you like church
the sun sets on my childhood home in july
looking back that's the last time it looked so bright
we didn't know that was summer's last song
the siren comes to an end
i was 8 years old
betting all my tokens this moment would happen again
we look to each other and rev our feet
this is my escape, where i go in my dreams

Expired Produce – Michaela Litwin (she/her)

there are rotting tomatoes in my fridge
& molding medallions on my skull
the scallions have gone bad
and it's only just spring
i'm struggling to make room for myself
in a life that is entirely mine
i'm complaining about the days slipping away
like it's a highway-fine
but the days belong to me
the minutes—all mine
i cannot keep saying i'm tired,
but it's all that i am
am i no longer poetry?
am i no longer artistic?
am i any less hungry,
for letting the produce expire?
am i no longer my most provocative-*selves*
because i am too tired?
the world needs saving & i need
fifteen more minutes of sleep
words are starting to feel stale
don't let my notepad become counter bread
you cannot shake people in an
ultra-tuned-in world
we are too tapped in
get me out
i want to be syrup

The Storm – Abu Ibrahim (he/him)

My sister told me there's been an unending storm in her city. It's been dancing around for days. Everyone has been advised to stay indoors. A drunk wind had ransacked her city. It's been roaming & leaving wreckage everywhere. She says her city looks like a dump site. The roof of her home is twirling in the air and her apartment is unrecognizable. All residents can do is look up to heaven. They are now hiding in the basement of a neighbours building. There people are bent in the posture of a prayer. She's been calling for help but no one is coming to save them. Nature cannot be appeased when outraged. Over the phone, I sat quietly listening to her speak. Her monologue is soundtracked by the wild howling of the wind. She lives in Middlesbrough and I'm in Lagos, and I am still shocked how she perfectly described the meteorological report of my life.

Ripples – David M. Alper (he/him)

She doesn't know the clouds will vanish, the water
will go down, and a drought will last for ten years.

If I ever felt overwhelmed by loss, your kiss
revived me. The girl keeps skipping stones,

always waiting for the ducks to be safe. The girl
skips stones by the lake, not looking back, not

knowing we're here in the tangled oak branches.
It feels like a different world, far away in time.

Like the ducks on her left, I've gone under the
surface and come back feeling more complete.

Like a water strider, we watch a rock skip across
the water, making ripples that spread.

She doesn't know love is as deep as this lake,
impossible to measure.

Green Reverie – David M. Alper (he/him)

A dull ossification and a brilliant *eau de Nil*
lodged in the roof, the drawers
of the hutch, the vices of the dining-room
tables: every facet of furniture
was covered with such a thin
green; the bright paper hung all about
like frozen blossoms. I loitered
in the gloom of the old house and tried
to measure its distance from the forest.
Here was everything which its sitters
sought; here was no visible subject
for Rimbaud, which is the subject of
The Tent.
Elsewhere, everything related to trees,
ferns, seashells, their names, but never to the
art or words, the ordinary subjects of writing.
I dreamed I told this idea to Rimbaud, that it was the
genre of his novels which gave him at last
this sort of subject for the art; I don't
know whether he knew any of my books, but
one day he asked me if I had ever
read the *Traité de l'Enseignement*
antique. I hadn't, but I was pleased to
tell him that, though I was so remote from
the plain truth about the *fin de siècle*.

Glimpses – David M. Alper (he/him)

trials up bitter glimpses
of other worlds beyond sight
glimpse long roads of gold
herbivore worlds
(plants, trees, grass)
glimpses
of dark worlds
(planets)
lungless breath
reaches for another sun
(stars)
the bower
of the pear
stale, touched
by memories
that rest on shelves
so even the spine is bent
and white as though
resting after the ultimate meal
in which you did not
abstain
you turned the key
and walked away
from the life
you'd known.

Dark Victory – Allison Whittenberg (she/her)

a good day is when a Betty Davis movie is on
because in the gold ole days
she real was the big one, bigger than Jean Arthur
she played it all
traumatizing
tantalizing
outrageous
spoiled
demanding
and always so memorable

Wonder why she dresses in limitations of black face for Halloween
for laughs
she claimed, as reminisce and spilled to Mike Douglas or was it, Merv
why?
this woman knew costumes—while in the MGM stable, she played everything
from the Queen (the Virgin) Elizabeth to a cockney whore <u>Of Human Bondage</u>
she played the old maid, but never the real maid

she was allowed range

and, all the glamor, as her eyeballs escaped their sockets (the unfair advantage of a thyroid condition),

so, she soared,
sad this proof exists on the internet
this dark victory

We know, Elsa – Allison Whittenberg (she/her)

after wedding Charles Laughton and playing the role of your life: a beard

how bad could Frankenstein's monster be
which one made your eyes great and glassy
which shot lightning streaks into your updo
which made you wail with fright

we know, Elsa, we know

Sopa De Letras – Zaira Gomez (she/her)

Metal Floral Engraving Clinks
Sifting,

                    B u s c a n d o

Around Wooden Blocks,

                    Mere Taut Reflection

Linking pedazos, letras

Memorias desde 6 años   soluciones para decir no suenos en
                                                                  el cielo
Destinos   deseos para decir si

Gather Tight Clusters
Present Apprehensively

As a wooden spoon
              They've already washed down the drain

Letters remain

Scraping stained sink
Rapidly saving them before

The last rinse gets them all

HEARD – Zaira Gomez (she/her)

Clamorous commands intwine red plastic indents
gripping squeals
Between sequences
"I may have something to tell you"
Past dusk mesh hazy dew morning
Sequences transition jagged spears
Spears coincide confessions
                "It's been going on for months"
Oh, so addiction

HEARD

A moment where desperation, redemption and salvation
Were singing from his tongue tied self
And the demons were roaming

Where past, present, future all present
Themselves in a moment of contemplation
Of divulgence

HEARD

The Memories My Eyebrows Hold – Aysha Siddiqui (she/her)

I hold the tweezers to my face
Plucking at the unruly parts of me
Until I no longer see my mother's daughter
Have I no land, no home, no birthplace?
I see the glistening pools of sadness in my eyes
At least that is mine, indisputable, it reminds me of what I am
Even if I've forgotten. The hot stove burning, the whirring of a fan
Passing a window, pausing in a hall,
a fruit-seller yelling, below me a colorful stall,
The smell of citrus mangoes drifting in
The monotonous sounds of daily routine, so loud and unfamiliar
And oh, how different even the crows look here
Grounded in reality, forming a memory
But it's already fading, and I'm no longer in Pakistan
The window is closed, it's silent now
And I'm already forgetting
The smell of mangoes
The hot air on my face
My grandma's cooking
Again, the pools in my eyes, is that all I am? a pool to reflect
what stands in front of me, morphing into where I am,
Now I look more like my friends that look nothing like me,
I'm a mirror of empty memory
Looking down the bathroom sink at the plucked hairs, I pause
Then turn on the faucet and watch the swirling water erase what
was

In My Mind Today – CLS Sandoval (she/her)

Too many entrances and exits
My anger convinces no one
If only I could see Chas again

The only thing left is food
I'm assuming the position to get there
And I'm not there

They said I was just too much
They said I was just too much
They said they wanted me to cut my hair
Wear different make up
Update my look

My anger convinces no one
Too many entrances and exits

**I'm afraid I have involved myself into something I'm not ready for –
Yuyi Chen** (they/them)

A pig has disappeared
and two and three
A man walks into the house of excrement
I smell ambition, a rumor...he says. he crinkles
when a prophecy is given:

There is a pignapper

First day of May the river shall dry
The higher the building, the
nastier the cloud
Who drops a hog's hair it makes a huge sound—
Oh, they send a brittle little man he
and all the cops
muffle the mayor; and load their guns

there   is   a   pignapper

To open a walnut the man spreads his palm
gullies explode a
continent flies
There is a foreign shadow stealthing away
The man catches it and he
announces:

The pignapper is on her way

Come crouch! Come fart! Come shake in the dark and familiar
yourself with the stench of women shrieking loud! Fire shots when
you are ready but be aware...these beasts...

these   beasts
the se   bea sts
t h es   ebe   asts

t h e s e v i c i o u s d e s i r e s a n d v u l g a r t e a r s

By the morning the building is gone;
First days of May the river overflows with fluffy honks
Emma Bovary rests in her most peace with pigs
The mayor passes out when he wakes;
I'm afraid,
I'm afraid,
I'm afraid I
have involved myself
into something I'm not
ready for.

One for breakup - Yuyi Chen (they/them)

Cats, or one of them culprits
has eaten the flowers you
brought to me

                                            The remaining buds would not die
                                            They dry up in front of windowsill
                                                        For months, months!

I
brought to
you

                                          Because we must exchange position
                                                       or a loss is not
                                                              a real loss

Your stiff stiff hands
hand me the purple bodies on the floor

                                                    The mom in my childhood
                                                devoured a dying cockroach

A washed room...
So the bed can float
everywhere the tear sheds

                                               Sleep is a labor of adulthood
                                                        My teeth cackle
                                                                  at night

Do I deserve this abundance?

                                                    I am no longer jealous

Do I burry you in the ceiling
like the girl I touched and lost?

                              I no longer kill my lover

We only get to have one second of truth
Then the lies
we are willing to hold
until they quiver and leak

                                           I
                                       No
                                   Longer
                                 Protest

Fourth of July, Another Day – Mark Kangas (he/him)

You sit in the waves and let them wash over you
kicked back with a pre-roll and sunglasses.
Red Ridge lips, I'm cooked on the sand
watchin' your back wet in a white tee
shaded by that blue bucket hat.
I see what you carry by the
slump of your shoulders.

Must There Be Valleys – Mark Kangas (he/him)

Finally,
found in the form
of flowers, in fireworks that flourish
from a lover's lips, we enter the honeymoon phase.
The grass is green, a decade of desire delivers the full menu by candlelight.
Earth tilting swings us through summer smooth as sailing, but our little labors of love
lull us asleep   as we reach   the peak   of a steep

                          slope

we plunge to the bottom of a valley where
we become our most demanding
we grow distant   coefficient
we budget the little time
we spend together
we see the end

loom

We refuse.

We go out for dinner Saturday night.
We look at each other's face more than we have in months and talk.
We bicker, banter, laugh it off. My obsessive mind slides past its usual hangups.

                                                       You smile.

I Never Hear Mention of the Caregiver – Mark Kangas (he/him)

there's no one else   you say
after going 'round and 'round
about dishes and weed and
having no privacy and hiding
your wallet and keys and how
sometimes you have to block
the number that keeps blowin'
up your phone when you are
working to pay for retirement
he'd end up dead in the street

We Don't Speak of That Sinking Feeling – Mark Kangas (he/him)

Torpedoes batter our hulls.
A lighthouse doesn't see.
Crews scurry to make repairs
below deck, out of sight.

Ghost ships clutter the harbor.
The coast guard arrives.
They call for tugboats.
They moor us in rows.

We cuddle in corners
of cold, unlit cabins
begging the war to end,
believing it never will.

They pull us out of the water
and put us in piles by a
sign reading KEEP OUT.
They wonder but don't ask.

Deep in the belly of a boat,
in the stillness of shock,
words of quiet desperation:

outside   *we can't*

**Voted the Best Spot for a Coffee and Joint in the Keweenaw –
Mark Kangas** (he/him)

Who voted, you?

That's the joke.

We sat on the driftwood bench you built between birch and pine, sheltered by leaf and needle with wind-shifting views filtering through of Superior and her waves giving one big *helloooooooooooooooooooooooooooooooo* far below.

Two votes, you and I.

Side-tracked - Claire Winter (she/her)

A moth flutters,
as if out of my own mouth—
glows in the sun.
The track-side alley
owns its flawed beauty.
I am received by it—
glimmered.
I wonder if
this is what death is like—
to be so enchanted

Diamond - Claire Winter (she/her)

I'm stuck here in a little world shrinking
pressed down on the head
brain clouded screen
time is in my eyes bright light
didn't used to bother me now I'm old
I fold myself in half to be things.
What is being?
Choice-making is what makes us human
right?

I don't choose choice I just do what I have to unless I can't
won't I want to be a solace but alas
I can't unravel myself and start
back re-making rubbing off edges,
wires, threads, needles all sharp pointy
scary and no good to a child
who had no choice
that was me not you, you know?

I just want to be like the others,
soft and lovely mummies,
but all the scary things, also
words that people said
brought me into being
something else folding,
shrinking not-choosing.

My Own Personal Pompeii – Jack Anthony (he/him)

What you have to understand is:
They didn't know.
They didn't even have a word for it.

The term *volcano* wasn't invented until the 1600s.
To the people of Pompeii, it was just a mountain.

It had been there all their lives, a fixed point,
looming in the distance and immutable in its enormity,
its nature.

'Til the tremors started, & the sky was choked with ash,
& red-eyed, chests heaving, the Romans discovered far too late:
the fiery river of Tartarus made real in their own backyards.

Perhaps they thought it divine punishment? Damnation
delivered Express by impatient Gods—a reflection of
human nature. Perhaps, face down on granite floors,
pleading, praying, they thought
why *me?*

As if this had never happened, as if they were
the first. When really, it was always inevitable,
boiling under the surface of unshakeable old Vesuvius.

That day the Romans learned you need not
know the name of the thing for it to burn you.

Do the Damn Dishes – Liz Bajjalieh (she/they/he)

Looking up towards the wooden moon
I saw the three cups of loss towering above
I snatched the greens from the ledge in the night
In hopes to protect them from the cold outside

And now there stands on the ledge what's left
I sit on the ground in grief
Washing dishes in the tub I usually keep as a spare drying rack
Filled with the drips of water I hoarded
To make sure the pipes don't freeze

I'm trying to do something
I want to be good
Here in the small moments I think of what's big

I think of spirits floating through Gaza
In a haze or prayer for tomorrow
Martyrs lay in the streets
After begging for a last breath under the rubble

I put my rubber gloves on
I look in the mirror and ask who I am
Stitched with the DNA of my grandfather
He was so proud of Ramallah
The Holy Land

So quiet as to all that he saw

I never knew him
But now I know the news
Of Khan Yunis and tears still after 100 days
Some made it this long, but don't know if they'll be here tomorrow
Netanyahu says the war will go on until 2025

What are these diasporic arms supposed to do?
US Senators stand in conversations, arms crossed
Smiling, after saying no to doing anything

The barrier of hell seems too sweet
Compared to all this, what's next beyond rage?

How far can the hand of greed reach into the heart?
They know what they're doing, but still they won't stop
It's a theory, a dream, a puzzle to solve

Eating up the little pieces like breakfast
While Gazans still starve
Racing towards promised trucks of food
Only to be shot down by IOF soldiers

I'm sitting in my grief
I look to the ledge
Bare of the green that once stood there
The plants I still tend to like children
It's where I try to hold on

Something to grab so I don't float away
I need to be here, rooted in the moment
We cannot let Gaza down, none of us

So do the damn dishes
Cry a million tears
Hurt with every cell of your being
This is what the world has come to
What we fought for and lost
And it is what you have to hold onto

Grasp it
Take a breath
Plant your feet like roots to the ground
Breathe, breathe
We hold our hearts and we work for liberation

A message for the modern-day colonizers – Liz Bajjalieh
(she/they/he)

And from the chaos of her throat
The woman sang,

"These were the grains of rice I told you to plant
At the heart of your soul. And what have you done?

Thrown them into your mountains of waste and said,
'I am the God of this tower
Crumbling beneath my feet.'
But you did not care of how it degraded, for now
At least you had a wide view
That stretched your supposed horizon
Further than the rest

But did you not learn your lesson?
The drums of time beat fast before you
Feel its tension, like the trigger of a gun
The slingshot you played with as a kid

You are a spec. Did you know? Did you see?
If you'd planted the rice, you would've then heard
The soft hum of earth and stone
The whispers she breathes from her chest

Instead you found oil
Not knowing that somehow within its black tar
Is eons of you and your blessed ancestors
Condensed into one flowing story

Can you imagine?
What could've been if you looked down
With the eyes of a child, wondering how many stars

Shined over the creatures you've made into plastic
Your alchemy is a hoax, no matter the past

Instead of beauty you made bombs for it
A wicked dream of dollar bills
That will only be but compost soon
Break down into nothing, but do you care?

Do you care at all?
Each moment holds an eternity
What magic life could be
If you'd live within the
wisdom
Of rice, of stars, and of stone."

Emergency Am I – Audrey Zee Whitesides (she/her)

The revolutions of emergency dancers
you see tonight
will perhaps remind you of your body
      but who's to say they won't
or will this reminder lead
      to productive fear?

I care,
trauma attention through price-checker
Popping out time
wants you madly, babe,
      pop me in the alley before you go

I want you to make me
make you breakfast on knees
      who else would I go to
now time cannot be
      managed humanely
      extralegal subject
      seem less violent than other

_____

distant state prod state
state state dry state
pull member turn member
state member speech member
end hairs imitate hairs
penalty hairs intimate hairs
force becomes harrow becomes
work becomes sadden becomes

I egged my distance
at you, it worked

Undercover at the Merch Table – Audrey Zee Whitesides (she/her)

Animal owners slip into dice rolls
blushing downwind at half-eaten fanfic
the unspeakable things those puppies do

Credit a blessing & condense into
accidental horror superfan
heavy robotic lips force a film
into first-person talk with implied response
leaving the meat to sit out
a few days, dieting in a nostalgic trench coat
trading ultraskin for a sexy September malaise

I forgot umbrella & my bluish lips
a special unbreakable voice
from the trees is a spell or curse
in the bedroom, missing one letter
& again after thought returned to thighs
every day flesh consumption
modified season, voice from a bone
curtain bangs & a sale dress in three parts
laboring, labored frame

A meal had me sweating in the car
like her mother
hounded velvet anywhere
but the forest
& the souvenir shirt makes a game
teen anger forever code
so when the seals & the sheets
bring an uproar to the back of the throat
it's a diamond-hard complicator
a pain that keeps me from holding my head up

Mirror Multiverse – Marcella Cavallo (she/her)

This is a holy place to cleanse your soul, not just your body.
It echoes your repressed feelings back to you.
Full confrontation, within four shiny walls, you can´t hide.

The bathroom floor turns into an open sky.
I always knew that tears melt tiles.
I fall and fall and fall.

And right in front of the mirror
I stop and float. Despite the invincible distance between us,
perhaps you wait on the other side?

I reach out, but there is no hand to pull me closer.
Nothing but a sharp silence that kills hope,
yet I step through the darkness

accompanied by my beating heart.
I can breathe in my pain and smell
the salt of my own ocean.

I always try to find answers close to water.
The white, thunderous horses will come and
break over me as I am

the shore, the cliff of my existence.
Peace will settle within me.
At least for a spark of time.

But they can´t bring back missed out moments,
they just carry taunting memories on their backs
and I am riding along with them.

Indifference – Daniel Schulz (he/him)

Chalk lines forming a picture frame.
Not perfect, critics morn.
Body cracked open by cement,
as if death were an act of artistry.
The crowd takes photos. I look above,
from hence he jumped,
and see angels watching us in awe.
The church bell rings, tells us the hour.
Compassion with wings of stone.

Untitled – Rachel Chitofu (she/her)

I'm nothing and everything at the same time,
Spilt water,
A wheel.
It's amazing
How I reel into places
That I shouldn't even
Be found.

Time has riddled me
Into a song
Of dead beetles,
Buried me
Underneath rivers
I shouldn't even be.

My hands,
Sculptures in their previous lives,
Have been chopped and ground
To chaff,
Diluted with carafe water.

My body,
Strained to sentences,
Bitter on your tongue.
Dust mingled
With bites of dust,
Only the bravest tears
Leave their mother,
The heaving cloud,
To rain on this land.

FICTION

Sigourney Weaver Comes to Movie Night at our Duplex – Liam Strong (they/them)

We're out of popcorn again, Gill. It's the seventeenth time this week, who knows in the month. Midge may die, I mean look at her—no, not her tail, don't let the wagging deceive you of happiness—just look at her. Look at me. Okay. I could possibly survive. It's one movie, maybe two. Whenever we fall asleep on the loveseat. Maybe we make it just one longer movie, like *Aliens*, *Alien 3* if we're feeling really masochistic tonight. It's this, the little survivals, the ones where we could die at any second because our needs aren't met.

By the way, are our needs not met? This seems to be the usual, our camp between two floral arms with the fibers fraying. Midge burrows, you know, or the couch has lost lower back strength, contracted by scoliosis, maybe an STD, who knows whose fault, but that's the least of our concerns. The biggest predicament is dinner.

At some point, fifteen minutes or an hour and fifteen minutes in, you spoil that the xenomorph was created as an analog for homosexual domination, gay oral, men like us dispersing spawn like parasites. There's transphobia too, but Ripley has a daymare of a baby xenomorph bursting from her abdomen before you get to that. My hand in your hand, exasperated, our conjoined hand up to my face to block the terror. Our hand an androgyny, our hand feeding us fear. My saliva an acid, but not the kind that melts, blood syrup from the alien, the proverbial unknown. Which is to say, Gill, that everything that carries safety can also carry our trauma.

Moreover, popcorn, Gill. Popcorn. It's aimless, the sex brought to my lips. And trust me—it's not you, it's not you. It's not you. We've run out of condoms, lube, and we're working with straws here. The headbite, inner jaw, the preferred method of killing, you say, isn't the alien's apparatus for consumption. Uncanonical, another synonym for us, but unconfirmed: maybe the xenomorph eats whatever it feels like. Whatever it needs, or doesn't need. It can choose starvation; it can choose fulfillness. Think of that, Gill, how we choose not what makes us full, but that we can be at all. And when, and how, and with whom.

I'm not a facehugger, not like I used to, not like when we slept over on third shift nights, our separate places, yours that old garage attic. The rent was cheap and we were richer because of it. As people, I mean. I hugged your face then like Smaug around his treasure, a serpent around certain kinds of organic fruits. When we can't sense thermal radiation, when our camouflage blends with the loveseat, when breath is forgotten. We used to tell each to breathe, to not be passive. Even Midge could tell when we'd be awake, nibbling at our earlobes.

Maybe the problem is that we need a new couch, need to make it smaller. If a two-seater is any less, though, where do we put feeling? If all I'm doing is touching you, consuming you, Gill, it's like I wouldn't be touching anything at all. That's how it works: we can't scream in space because no one hears us. So we're not screaming at all. Like we don't have neighbors, or have too many, or the walls are thin enough that your father a state over can hear us fucking. Is it everyone else we fear, the noises we make, the crunch and pop of something delicious that could, in the end, be bad for us?

That love, too, could be toxic to us?

Maybe the problem is also that Ripley fears love, loving, its adjacencies, off-shoots, and spin-offs. She is often the strongest and weakest character all at once, Gill, but I like to think that the viewers take part in this competition as well (Midge, of course, the only one really paying attention, ears poised for jumpscares, and squished between our laps, is the strongest character in our story).

Because at the end of *Aliens*, the decimated crew dies disgusted at the xenomorph, the so-called perfect being that is in no way godlike, and yet exudes the horror of one. You're an essayist when you're left to your own head, lover, but even when Ash reveres the xenomorph in *Alien*, we're still left with immorality in our mouths. The couch wants to devour us whole, hide our bodies from who loves or once loved us. We could stay here forever, then. We could stay here, and the universe would be none the wiser, because a couple of lazy fags won't rescue a crew of space militants from dying.

The horror isn't that we'd probably die too, nor would it be that the xenomorph isn't the true villain. It's the unseen cast, the government, the world—whoever you want to give names to, Gill. If we could fear with full eye contact, then we might as well fuck, no love necessary, but within reach of cushions. We can be disgusted, we're allowed to, we're allowed to be fulfilled by disgust. We could get the cheapest, most synthetic popcorn from the corner store in our pajamas, the kind that no seasoning could save. We could die by our own diseases, our own kind, but at least we can buy fulfillment for just a few bucks. We could leave the kernels in our gums, sharp imitations of fangs, so that nothing will ever taste bad again. We don't even need to brush our teeth afterward.

First published in miniskirt magazine

Additional Supernatural Discoveries of the Dog Meadow Light, Circa 2022 – Liam Strong (they/them)

Please. It's for research, Gill. Research! Even if the Paulding Light already has several confirmed debunkings, I want to contribute more. And no, I won't find a more popular paranormal hotspot, and no, don't you dare call it a coldspot, you're not as funny as you think you are, except you are, and no, I won't pick a place closer for my birthday. The day I was birthed into the world, my body red and bituminous with firedamp. I swear I would jump out of this Honda right now if we had better life insurance.

We're near the Wisconsin border, where my mother was born, but I don't know where. For all we know we're at the wrong crevice of the state. Michigan doesn't feel like a bridge because it isn't. Michigan doesn't feel like a special place where special shit happens, but that's why this is special, Gill. Perhaps, and take note, the thesis of all birthday culture. That we manifest the special energy, plop it into a gift, and then we end the day with some orgasms. It's easy, really, maybe too easy, but it's easy to be this special, or not, but it's easy to think otherwise, a couple and their sheepdog with the backseat all to herself, the normalcy of what's special.

Which, of course, makes a place like Paulding go from unspecial to special in the flash of a light! Your favorite conclusion—no, let me guess—isn't that the phenomenon in Paulding is a product of automobile headlights careening from a perfect angle on US 45. No, I think you're into the swamp gas theory, probably because it sounds both funny and plausible all at once. It's valid, checks out, at least for you, Gill, your logic as bulletproof as a ghost. I can see it on your face, the embarrassment, simply from me knowing, but that could be what makes our particular folklore, for lack of a better term, special.

You see, Gill. Well, you see too clearly. Everyone needs glasses these days, so maybe I'm plagued by tricks of the eye. Virgin forest blurs into stoneface up here, beyond the Straits of Mackinac, the sky and stars too close for comfort. And I thought cities were claustrophobic. You see things for what they are and nothing else, because really, nothing else is there. You, me, Midge, an unpaid car with a loan from your aunt, the last one you have, a Coleman cooler with a few Sprites or Sierra Mists. It feels like there's miles between all of those things. Because there aren't.

***

The grandparent's lantern needs more oil. The railroad brakeman's flashlight dies while attempting to save a train from a head-on collision. An indigenous woman dancing along the powerlines, each fracture of starlight just another question to be asked. A vacationing dogman from Wexford County holding a rave before he has to go home again. A college girl and her soon-to-be ex-girlfriend, her laptop with porn flickering like a silent film chopping up the night.

Really, Gill. Light can come from anything.

***

There's light in Paulding during the day too, Gill. Lots of it. Not just from the sun, but from people, refracting leaves, snow if the sheets are flat enough. The Paulding Light is any explanation you want it to be, you dummy. You have to let things be the difficult answer, the gift that challenges you, even if you don't feel good giving it. That's not the point. I want you—I need you—to see something that makes your face brighten anxiously with something unexpected. Even if it's a maple tree at the distant mouth of the valley where every firefly in the Upper Peninsula congregates, a tenement house or church of glowing, shameless insects, unafraid of being seen. Even if it's a match I have to keep hidden from you the whole trip, just to watch it disappear again. Even if I have to imagine your reaction in the darkness leftover.

There Was Never Anything to Forgive – Liam Strong (they/them)

I won't force the metaphor, Gill. I'll leave the question hanging there for you, when you come back home, the corner lamp left dim. My bracelet is still on. I normally take shit like that off when I shower or sleep or fuck. On a hierarchical scale, fights can be wars, can be battles, can be skirmishes, can be just about anything you'd name on a thesaurus website. I'm not using the words like or as.

/

The Akhmatova quotes excommunicated to the region of the freezer handle. I call the paper scraps edgy and you unstitch all the pockets in your end of the closet like kidneys from a ribcage. In return, I leave you love letters under your pancakes written by yourself. It's a pure kind of evil, not pure evil. We go back and forth, which is a kind of fucking, which I didn't know could happen without the act, the event, the pomp and parade. We remove the bed from the bed when we're angry. I told my mother about you once in a dream of hers that she texted me about at 5 A.M. I wish I knew what she had said, but also don't.

/

You left the lamp on after you came, while you slept, as you left. It has never been turned off, Gill. I'd like to believe that, so I will.

/

Before we moved in, another couple lived there. I don't know if they were gay, though. I don't know if the couple before us knew if the couple before them were gay, either. If the grand-couple were gay, which they probably were, they wouldn't have known if the god or gods they believed in were gay. There is an unrelenting train with passenger seats full of emptiness. It sounds impossible, but it isn't.

/

The silkworms and milkweed bloomed at the same time this year, which means we'll have to keep doing the same old shit in the same old place. I'd like to have options. Or at least a benchmark, a reasonable reason for change, a changeable change, one that seems doable, within the range of our bodily functions and mental health. Gill, the magnets say everything otherwise, a language we can't parse even though it's in our mothers' tongues. Your favorite one, the favorite because it's stupid, so stupid, so great, so great it's stupid, about how the salmon aren't running this season. I believe you aren't stupid because I believed it. We're stupid until proven otherwise, forgivable until our names are taken away from us. I've given us our all and I'll do it again until we feel like less is also enough. I replaced my kneecaps with bottle caps to make a joke before, because the laughter peeked into the kitchen looking for you. In the middle of the apartment is another apartment, and we're always on the edge of what could be. Our pity might just be that, Gill, edging and edging. Since the salmon can't run without feet, can't swim without being between the edge of water and sunlight. And just being okay with that.

Bugs – Abhishek Udaykumar (he/him)

Litha cried when the gardener trimmed the mango tree. She sat in the kitchen with her ginger drink and wiped the dishes to distract herself, staring vacantly through the back window. It had been a month since the bushfire and the shrubs had begun to sprout, growing urgently in the fragmented manner that life had assumed since the start of summer. She thought about her secluded world beneath her mango tree where she had spent her mornings trying to read, waiting for the water to come so she could bathe. The tree had stopped fruiting, sucked the nutrition out of the soil, and needed more water than she had for herself. She would step out once the gardener had left and look at it from a distance.

The evening waned into a waxy candle. The house sat on the outskirts of the town—a dry, eggy cottage in the middle of a scrubland. She used to work as a nurse in the local hospital; after years of study, her first job brought her closer to the people in ways that she couldn't have imagined. She no longer remembered if the choice had always been her dream, or if her circumstances had morphed her desire till it was all she had known. Eventually, it wore her out—she wanted to read and write again. She finished her drink and rocked herself in the living room, glaring into space till her presence horrified her. She changed out of her skirt and shirt and wore an old onesie and a high pony. The gardener was separating the branches from the leaves. He would carry them home and use them in ways that she did not know. The idea of arranging a butchered tree into neat piles aroused a strange sensation within her and she paced about the house despite the heat and dwindling daylight.

She locked up and left the house through the backyard. The back gate opened out to a slope of thorny bushes that surrounded a sandy ravine. A path running along the slope led further away from the outskirts to an endless patchwork of fields. The world around her was brown, and a sheet of purply, cottony sky stretched beyond the thistles and forest of branches. Puddles of water hugging the foot of the ravine broke into brief streams and ended before they could become a river. She smiled at the triangles of birds flying back home, gripping a bucket and a large mug fashioned out of a plastic can. The highway would appear at the mouth of the ravine, where an old dam held the water on the other side when the rains finally came. But she wouldn't go that far. There was a clearing where the ravine caved into a shallow sandbank, letting her slide along its gentle slope, until she found herself beside a pond and an archipelago of puddles.

The silence made her feel like the only human on earth. Its apparent ubiquity enlivened her presence, like a rare wildcat enamoured by its own mystique. She felt her skin, her muscles, her nails and her wispy hair pulsing in the sultry earthen heat of the mudbank. It awakened her senses and urged her body into action; she felt like she was watching herself, enchanted by her movement and gaze. She slipped her feet beneath the frilly water, and it consumed her with eager indifference. As though she was but a stone, a twig or a seed. She skirted along its shallow edges, making ribs in the sand with her bare toes. Then she looked up at the sky again, smiling and turning back to the pond. She picked up her pail and ran it across the water, stretching into the deeper regions to avoid the fish and tadpoles that tickled her feet. When she had filled three-quarters of the bucket, she hurried up the slope and began to pour it along a stretch of saplings. She had planted them after the bushfires and she hoped to turn them into trees with the water that she had found in the ravine.

There were forty saplings in all. She had bought them at a horticulture sale in the bazaar and had hired a pickup truck to deliver them home. It had taken her two weeks to plant the saplings. They seemed to have taken kindly to the soil, except a few that had wilted partially. She had dug a well around each sapling to ensure that the water didn't wander back to the pond. When she was done inspecting them, she returned to the pond, filled her bucket and hurried back up the slope.

She thought about her routine over those two weeks—she would go to the pond with her spade after breakfast and water the soil for a few hours, loosening it till she could dig a row of pits. She would then bring the saplings three at a time on her wheelbarrow, before breaking for lunch beneath a clump of acacia – the only trees that offered any shade in the scrubland. It had felt long enough to be a summer holiday; she had grown fond of it and begun to believe that it wouldn't end. By night, she would be too tired to cook, and she would eat a basket of fruit and drink a tall glass of cold milk before falling asleep on the sofa. She would sleep a dreamless sleep and wake up feeling a pleasant ache in her muscles, the joy of making something grow pulsing inside her chest. She would eat as abundantly as she could and scurry across the ravine to her plants. A bottle of water and a lunchbox In her bag.

She sat beside a tamarind sapling and inspected its leaves. The plant had begun to seek its independence from her and she started to sing *A Whole New World* as she patted the mud. The evening rotted like a wounded peach, but Litha was brimming with life. She did a little dance and returned to the pond to tell her stories to the fish and the frogs that missed her laughter in the frightful night.

On the way back, she found a cluster of ladybugs making their way up the trunk of an old, barren tree. She stood there with her hands on her back, watching them flutter with purpose as they ascended the woody veins. Their red bodies seemed out of place in the featureless land, and the little black spots on their backs were comical as though they belonged to a silly board game. She used to collect them when she was a child and put them into jars with holes punched into their lids. She would place a large twig, a few leaves, and a little grass inside for the beetles to climb; but despite reading about them for hours in encyclopedias, she didn't know where to find the right food. She would eventually let them out where she had found them and spend the evenings following them, imagining her garden to be a planet of its own and the beetles its inhabitants.

The light had withdrawn from the world, turning her into an apparition smudged against a charcoal landscape. She was helpless against the tide of time and insignificant amongst nature's many creatures. A wave of sadness shrouded her as she made her way back home, sticky and lost in her lonesome world. The water that had once filled the ravine and gurgled through her dreams had turned into a mere secretion of the earth. Another arid month and the soil would begin to crack, chasing the farmers and their cattle up the hills to seek the cool promise of clouds. The fields 104ouldd roll into themselves like ragged cloth and reveal the parched skeleton of land beneath. Summer had just begun and her trips to the pond were becoming arduous with each day.

She drifted past the back gate and washed herself with the bucket she had filled that morning; the water level had dropped, and the surroundings showed signs of four-legged visitors in her absence. She slumped against the backdoor, drawing her legs along the warm concrete steps and stone ground . She undid her hair and tied her ponytail as high as she could, turning to the bats and cranes that ruled the sky as night lounged behind the whale skin sky. She was camouflaged in the musky evening and stared hard at the objects around her house, trying to recognize them in the chocolatey dark. A pack of wild dogs howled beyond the clearing, and boars nodded along the ravine like legendary monsters. There was no sign of people, though the town had grown and felt closer than it had when she was a child. The current was out, and she didn't dare enter the house till the fans could be switched on. She leaned against the doorway and thought about the ice cream she had bought a few days ago, and how it must have turned to milk in her poor refrigerator. Life was real only as long as she lived, but the ladybugs didn't know that, and they sprinted across anything that nature laid them upon; the idea almost made her laugh.

She stood up and slowly made her way around the house, past the old garage and the living room window, till she found herself in the front yard. It was too dark now to see the houses beyond the compound sloping down the formless land. A car snaked along in the distance and zipped the baglike valley, and nothing was visible after it passed. But Litha could see the dilapidated branches of her mango tree despite its lack of leaves. She felt a rush of sympathy in her crusting throat for memories lost in vivid lanes of summers and mango days. "It would grow back," the gardener had said, but Litha was beyond comfort. She swallowed and held herself together till she was beneath its sprawling body, the lower branches feathering her hair with its thinning bouquet of leaves. She looked up in anticipation and imagined the familiar thicket of her tangy green tree, but all she could see was the moonless sky through its leafless arms. She hugged its trunk, closed her eyes, and let the tears break through her again till she began to shiver.

Buses – Abhishek Udaykumar (he/him)

This time Kanai got off. He circled the sleepy depot and returned to the parking lot. It was quiet beside the highway. The little town beyond the terminus chattered as the sun waited patiently between the horizon and the other side of the world. Its syrupy light enlivened everything and turned the cotton candy sellers and chirpy conductors to brassy beings. His legs had stiffened along the way, and there were five hours to go. He could have taken the air-conditioned train, but the road journey helped him see the world; with his old camera and faded blue jeans—he seemed to be in search of an idea, or dereliction.

An old orange bus swerved off the country road and parked inside the terminus. It was crowded as it was bound for the city; the standing travelers shuffled out slowly before the crumpled passengers unfolded from their seats. The station seemed momentarily confused till the people scattered to the refreshment stalls. A boy stepped out with his younger sister, a bundle of bags around his shoulders. He asked his sister to sit with their things while he got them a bottle of water.

Kanai stared at a woman washing her face with a bottle. Three men on a scooter rode into the depot to pick up a friend. The boy and his sister seemed to have travelled a long distance, and they didn't have the energy to speak. Kanai wandered to the end of the terminus, becoming smaller as he reached the greasy bus bay where drivers slept beneath their buses. He thought about his last project and the adventurous months in the village. A part of him had wanted to stay, but the slowness of life there made him long for the city despite its fleeting nature. Eventually, it led to more disillusion, making him long for the mountains again.

The girl had become restless. She asked her brother to buy her a cone of *churmuri*[2] and he reluctantly agreed. He sighed and gazed

---

[2] A popular South-Indian street food made with puffed rice, roasted peanuts, raw onions, tomatoes, carrots and spices.

at the bus before he pulled out a journal and a few pens. Kanai had circled the depot for the second time and when he returned, he saw the boy sketching the evening world around them as it wrestled gracefully with the coming twilight. It drew Kanai towards the siblings till he was peering into the boy's book, his sister looked up as she picked her *churmuri*. It was a side view of the terminus with a family leaving through the gates—the woman carried a suitcase on her head while the man's bag was too big for him; their children scuttled along, oblivious to the world's troubles.

It was a while before the boy looked up with a shy smile. He averted his face and went back to his drawing. Kanai went around the bench to get a better look, and the little girl followed him with her eyes. The drawing was imperfect but original; it had an eye for character and avoided unnecessary detail. Kanai was aware of his proximity to the sketch. He didn't fancy himself as a spectator, and he wasn't sure of what to do with his hands. The girl was still watching him with big obnoxious eyes, whispering to her brother as she tossed the *churmuri* through her lips.

"Will it be dark when we reach home, *bhaiya*[3]?" she asked. He didn't reply and she grew irritable, "people keep staring at you."

The boy tried to hush her, aware of Kanai and a few others who had begun to watch him draw. Kanai considered getting onto the bus, but his captivation had turned to curiosity. The girl shifted and spilt some of the dry mixture as she tried to tie her hair. The boy turned briefly but refused to clean up. She stood up frustrated and prepared to throw the whole thing when she slipped on the mess and dropped the cone on her brother's lap. He was quick to get his book out of the way, but his tolerance had been tested, and he pulled her back into the bus.

Kanai could see the lights come on in the little town. A series of yellow and white dots skirted the skyline, and a mosque began to sing. There were more people marching into the bus stand with plastic sacks and wire baskets tucked under their arms. The women

---

[3] The Hindi word for brother.

were wearing dense silk *saris*[4] with garlands curled around their hair. Everything was an occasion in India. The boy returned after a long while. He had left his things on the bus, but it didn't matter now because the light had diminished and there were buses grinding into the terminus. The world had changed in his brief absence. He sat down and crossed his knees. Kanai wandered up to him and began to speak, swallowing his words at first before starting over.

"How long have you been drawing?" he said, instantly furious at himself for the mundane question. But the boy seemed to be unaware of such speculation. He smiled again and spoke thoughtfully, looking Kanai in the face.

"It's good time pass. I always used to draw, but these days I am carrying it everywhere." The boy seemed like a North-Indian so Kanai decided to switch to Hindi and not bother him with English.

"You have a really good...You're good at depicting pictures. You have a way of knowing how to depict the important things in a picture."

The boy smiled at himself and looked away. He preferred being polite, though he never denied a compliment.

"So, are you studying or...?" A common Indian question. Once again Kanai was annoyed by his own thought process.

"I finished my Mass Comm, and now I'm looking for a job." He was quiet for a few moments, watching passengers hover around his bus and wondering if he should go back. "But it's difficult to find one these days."

"Yeah..." Kanai had never had a job, but he understood strife in his own way. The boy asked him what he was doing.

"I'm a writer. I'm a writer and an artist." Kanai was hesitant about telling people that he was also a filmmaker. But the boy's eyes were glistening already and they urged him to say more. "And I make films as well."

---

[4] A garment that consists of a long cloth worn by women in the Indian subcontinent.

"Short films?" the boy was excitable now, though he was making a great effort to subdue himself.

"Not really, actually. I make longer ones."

The boy stood up and balanced himself between the platform and the parking lot, his hands on his hips.

"That's great, I have been working on a script as of late for a short film. I've made one small film so far. Just a five minute one, and I put it on YouTube."

Kanai did his best to reciprocate the boy's enthusiasm, but he felt dazed when he met people who claimed to make films. The boy had started to fiddle with his phone, trying to get his video to open despite the poor network.

They found themselves obstructing the passengers and moved back to the bench. The video had begun to play, launching a dramatic sequence of people scurrying around a lakebed carrying saplings and buckets of water, buffering periodically. The music was loud, the narration was lost in the crowding depot, and though the language was familiar to Kanai, he was unable to process the film. The frames were thoughtful, which was a relief, unlike several amateur filmmakers who shot mindlessly in order to expand their repository. It was a documentation of a tree-plantation drive, organized by a local NGO. The breeze brought the conductors to life as they yelled for passengers, chanting the names of destinations. The night was sinking in, and the video seemed to go on forever, the boy sticking his arm out and gleaming at the radiant screen, till the lights above them came alive and the phone lost its three-dimensional effect.

The ending was overdone. The montage was too quick and it was clear that his client had coaxed him into mashing a great deal of information inside a fixed duration. The slow-motion effects, stylized transitions and catchy fonts at the start of the sequence ended with what looked like a biology textbook. It was meant to be a promo, but the spirited boy had tried to make a film out of it. Kanai smiled warmly as he remembered his first attempts at making a film. The boy's video was a gospel of flaws for first-timers.

"It was nice," he said, unsure of what else to say to the beaming boy. 'It was nice."

"What about your films? Are they online?"

"Hmm, no. They aren't. I usually screen them."

"What?"

"Umm..." People were unfamiliar with the idea of a screening. Kanai decided that he had explained it too many times in the past.

"I don't put them online," he repeated. "The trailers and archives are online though."

"Oh." The boy was disappointed. He seemed to have understood in his own way.

"So, did you study filmmaking?" he asked.

"No, I didn't." More of the uncomfortable terrain.

"Oh?"

"I studied art."

"Painting?"

"Yes, yes." He had persevered, on several occasions, to explain that he had studied Contemporary Art, but he had given up a long time ago and had begun to believe that it wasn't different from visual art, or fine art, or just art. His degree didn't exist in the wider Indian vocabulary.

The boy was impressed. Kanai wanted to change the subject. He would soon have to tell him that he had studied abroad. It was tiresome enough that he knew about his filmmaking. He felt that filmmakers were seen as people of power and that the medium had become a form of authority with little aesthetic and individuality.

"What kind of films do you make?"

"I've made some documentaries, and a few fiction films. These days I've gotten more into fiction, but I wanna get back to documentaries soon."

"So you write your own scripts?"

"Hmm, sort of. I don't really write scripts. I just follow my instinct."

"Oh...I see."

"What about you? What else do you do?" Kanai felt himself looking around, as though he were simply echoing the world's questions.

"I finished college a year ago, but my father is finding it difficult to work these days, so I do a nightshift at a call center. It's been six months now, and I'm still looking for a job, or work in a production house, maybe as a videographer. I'm trying to build my portfolio."

Kanai knew the story. It was a result of the country's dysfunctional education system and its irrelevance to employment. It was a populated country, but its people had immense capability. They just didn't have the opportunity.

Necessity and economy trumped art and turned it inside out till it resembled a utility like most other things. But art remained on the inside if one looked long enough. The boy's visual language was promising, and he had a touching perception of moments. Kanai was weary and wanted to disappear. The loneliness he had suffered over the years seemed insignificant in comparison to the boy's isolation from the art world.

"So where are you going now?"

"Back to Bangalore. We have an uncle who lives in Hassan, and we came to visit him because it was a long weekend."

"Oh, I live in Bangalore too."

"Which part?"

"Sarjapur."

"Oh, that's not too far from where I live," the boy mused, wondering if this meant anything. "Are you travelling by yourself?"

"Yeah. Yeah. Just travelling. I just finished a film and I wanted a break from the city, you know? It's too much. So, I'm going to Chikmagalur. Just to explore."

The boy didn't know where that was. He grew distracted as the bus filled up; he wanted to go back to his sister. He smiled, nodded his head and laughed a little, not wanting to break away first. Kanai felt bitter and looked at his feet, smearing the floor with his boots. The idea of hard work was a fallacy. Everybody worked hard. But success wasn't a result of hard work. The demands of capitalism allowed for success if an individual tailored their existence to suit those demands.

The glaring lights of the bus station had snatched the charm from everything. It reminded them that it was another public place, and their memory of it would linger, if at all, as a quiet image once they had passed. The vividness of the depot made them weary as people and things bunched into empty spaces. The town had vanished from their view as vehicles swam into the darkened distance, the pithy lamplights glimmering along the way like vague reminders of day. The driver climbed into his seat and combed his hair, lighting a fresh *bidi*[5]. He sounded his musical horn and made them tremble as people peeped out of their windows and thought about something or someone.

He watched the boy trying to make his way into the orange bus and thought about the final paragraph from *The Postmaster* by Rabindranath Tagore.

"So, the traveller, borne on the breast of the swift-flowing river, consoled himself with philosophical reflections on the numberless meetings and partings going on in the world—on death, the great parting, from which none returns."[6]

---

[5] An unfiltered form of a cigarette rolled into a bidi leaf instead of paper.
[6] The Postmaster, Rabindranath Tagore, East Bengal, 1891.

Kanai reflected on his behaviour and wondered if he could have been a better person. He felt a pang of guilt because he couldn't help the boy. He could barely help himself. And yet he could have offered more of himself if he had tried. Kanai clenched his lips and quivered with regret. The nonsensical horn bellowed for the second time and the remaining passengers hopped in, hanging from the door in a pile. The bus had swallowed the boy and his sister and began to reverse out of the parking lot. Kanai stood by himself, gripping his phone like a bat, watching the bus tilt out of the depot. He shut his eyes and relived his memory of the siblings, innocent and human on the lukewarm planet. If only he had participated with more zeal. It didn't matter that he was an artist, a filmmaker, or a writer. It didn't matter unless it involved sharing a portion of himself. But the idea had formed a little too late. And his bus to the mountains would soon be off, further than where memory could mean anything beyond an extinguished pellet of time.

Pink Vanity – Toshiya Kamei (they/them)

The trouble is that reflections are deceptive. A mirror reverses what's in front of it.

I would mime in front of my mother's vanity-table mirror, pointing at the plain girl staring back. My reflection would mimic me like an obedient twin. Although puberty blockers lessened my anxiety, a hint of insecurity flashed in her dark eyes.

One day, to my astonishment, my reflection moved in the opposite direction. The light played tricks on me and our two reflections overlapped. I gasped. In that moment, I felt whole and somehow truer than before. When my reflection moved again, the sudden loss burrowed into my chest.

At first, I found all this amusing and kept entertaining myself with my reflection like before. However, the girl in the mirror grew rebellious over time. She no longer obeyed me when I started high school, and she dyed her hair pink. My reflection would move of its own accord, and cold sweat would run down my spine. My only relief was that the other me remained trapped in the mirror.

Sometimes my reflection talked to me.

"Call me Alexa," she said.

"Alexa." I swallowed. She was pretty—prettier than I was.

"Do you have a problem with that?" she asked. There was an edge to her tone.

"My friends and family call me Lexi," I said. "Choosing my name was important for me."

"I know," she said. "It's my turn to choose mine."

I remained silent, looking down.

"I can taste your craving for me," she said, and I looked up. Tears filled my eyes.

"What's the matter?" Alexa said. Her words cut like knives. "Why don't you admit how much you want to be me?"

I ran upstairs, skipping steps, and locked myself in my room. I flopped on my bed, covered my head with the coarse cover, and trembled in silence.

Since then, I've kept my distance from the vanity table.

One Sunday evening, I told my mother about the other me, but she thought I was pulling her leg.

"You're not a teen idol, Lexi," my mother said. "Why would anyone pretend to be you?"

If I winced, she didn't notice. I didn't have the answer to that either.

"Forget it, Mom," I said, kissing her goodnight.

The following day, thoughts of Alexa distracted me. In my daydreams, I pressed my hand into the mirror, and Alexa yanked me in. Laughing, she put my hand in her mouth. When she swallowed me, I pulsed in the warm dark.

"Lexi, did you hear about the latest kaiju attack?" Jorge said when he walked into the classroom and sat next to me, brushing his curly bangs away from his brown eyes. "Pasadena this time."

I shrugged with disinterest. Like everyone else, I was sick of useless lockdown drills. The worst part was that some teachers forced kids to use buckets as toilets. If a kaiju attacked our school, we'd all die anyway.

"Why did you act so weird at the mall yesterday?" Jorge asked. "And I tried to text your new number, but you didn't answer."

I frowned. "I wasn't there yesterday. You know I work at the café on the weekends. And I don't have a new number."

My eyes widened at the hurt in his. "Now you're lying to me," he said. "It had to be you. But you did have pink hair. Was that a wig?"

Pink hair. *Alexa*. I was speechless. I gripped the desk until my fingers hurt. She was out of the mirror. But how?

It made no sense. What did she want?

"Lexi? Are you okay?" Jorge waved a hand in front of my face. He held his phone in his other hand. "Look. I took a picture of you, but it's kinda fuzzy."

Intense lighting shone on her heavily made-up face, and dark glasses rested on her pink hair. She wore a white tank top with a fuchsia skirt tightly hugging her hips. She had my face.

Fear skittered up my spine.

"That's not me, Jorge," I said. "I'd never dress like that."

"Yeah right," Jorge scoffed, licking his rosy lips.

When I ran to the bathroom during recess, my reflection was my own again. Alexa was gone. I didn't know what was worse—my terror or my disappointment.

***

"Your cousin in Osaka thinks it's a mirror curse," my mother said across from me at the dinner table. I hadn't seen Alexa in a month. By this time, Mom had come to entertain the possible existence of my double.

"You can ask Ayaka next week. She's coming to stay with us for the summer."

Ayaka was an occult maniac. She'd talk your ear off about poltergeists once she got started. We were the same age but had little in common. I was afraid I'd be her chauffeur all summer because she didn't drive.

On Friday afternoon, I drove to the airport and waited for Ayaka. I spotted her easily in the crowd because she was the only one masked. She dipped her head in a slight bow. I offered a shy smile. She wore blue jeans, a white T-shirt, and a blue summer jacket. Contact lenses tinted her eyes light pink. Unlike me, she'd grown taller since I last saw her.

"Mirrors distort you, Lexi," Ayaka said as we drove home.

"Excuse me?"

"The universe is out of whack," Ayaka said, taking a water bottle from her backpack. "Thanks to humans destroying the Earth, kaiju are awakening and people are being haunted by their doubles. It all leads back to climate change."

"What should I do? Should I talk to Alexa? Jorge gave me her number."

"No!" Ayaka glared at me. "Don't ever do that!"

"Why?" I asked, taken aback.

"You're not supposed to interact with your doppelgänger. It's too dangerous."

"What will happen?"

"The world may collapse for all I know."

I said nothing.

***

Ayaka and I sat before the mirror in my mother's room. Everything seemed ordinary, except that I looked paler than usual.

"What do you think?" I asked, frowning at my reflection.

"We're looking at a portal to another dimension," Ayaka said as she touched up her lip gloss.

"My doppelgänger came through that?" I asked, still incredulous.

"That's right." She nodded.

I kept quiet.

"Remember that video I sent you a few weeks ago?" she asked.

"The Zelenskyy look-alike in Osaka?"

Ayaka nodded again.

"He came through a portal," Ayaka continued. "The real Zelenskyy was visiting Osaka."

"The doppelgänger wanted to meet him," I said.

"But I destroyed the portal before their paths could cross."

"Do you mean the digital camera you broke?" I asked. "That was a portal, too?"

Ayaka shrugged. "My dad grounded me for a month, but I had no choice."

I had no idea how the Ukrainian president felt about his double, but I wanted to be Alexa. She was a better version of me.

"The thinning ozone layer has caused portals to open," Ayaka said. "I don't know how many there are, but we're in constant danger."

I tore the skin around my nails. Danger. I recalled the moment when I merged with Alexa in the mirror—the dizzying sense of relief I felt, the freedom. How could feeling free be that dangerous? Why was wanting to be with her wrong?

"Aren't you hungry, Aya-chan?" I asked, calling her by her childhood nickname to hide my irritation. Even after her warnings, I wanted to be united with my double. I felt like giving in and risking everything. "I'm starving."

I went downstairs into the kitchen to fix a snack.

"Alexa." Her name escaped my lips as I reached for a bag of chips on the top shelf. My desire for her seized me, and I could no longer resist. I stepped outside and dialed Alexa's number with trembling fingers. The evening sky turned magenta. I felt someone behind me. When I turned, it was me. Or rather, the other me.

"Hi, Lexi." Alexa smiled. My whole body shook with excitement. Unable to contain myself, I stepped forward and embraced her. It felt like coming home.

The hiss of the window sliding open made me look up. I gasped. Her arms straining, Ayaka tipped the vanity-table mirror off the sill. Worry flashed in her eyes for a moment before the triumph took over. I turned to Alexa, and there was fear in her gaze for the first time. As the mirror hit the concrete patio and shattered, she drew me tighter. My cry was drowned out by the smash.

Fresh night breeze caressed my face, and the sky was devoid of magenta. Ayaka was coming. Her footsteps stormed down the stairs. I crouched and picked up a shard of glass. The surface was smudged with blood, but I wasn't sure if it was mine or Alexa's. As I searched for a reflection in the glass, I wasn't sure who I expected to find.

Lake Melliza – Daniel Deisinger (he/him)

Katie glanced around at the empty road, then forged through the trees. Sharp wind cut across her cheeks, and her boots kicked up small snow puffs. She slid down the slope; pine needles rained around her as she stopped herself on a tree. Glancing at her watch, she kept walking until the hard, shimmering surface of Lake Melliza appeared in front of her.

She brushed past a small warning sign and put half her weight on the ice. It held steady. Her other foot trailed behind. Only howling wind reached her ears as she stood on the frozen bank. Polished ice reflected trees, dense clouds, and her own hurrying form as she scurried across.

She kept her eyes on the stone skyscraper looming over trees on the other side, heading straight toward it. The lake cracked. The sound filled the empty air over the lake. Katie stopped, heart beating in her throat. Nothing but her confused expression looked back from under her. Shaking her head, she rushed forward, grumbling to herself. Her boots glided against the lake as she pumped her arms.

Again, she checked her watch, and something shifted below. Fish? Still, only her reflection, just as confused, stared back at her.

Her reflection bent down, driving its fingers up through the ice into fresh air, grasping for her foot. Cold water bubbled through from under the ice.

Katie jumped back. Her duplicate stayed in place. The two Katies locked eyes, and then the reflection smiled. It rose, feet planted on the underside of the ice, and dove forward before Katie could react.

Her back slammed against the ice, and a deep crack echoed around her. The clouds spun above; a crown of pain radiated from the back of her head. She tore her boot out of the ice-cold grip and scrambled away, trailing dots of red blood on the frozen surface from her knees. Another crack shifted the ice. Freezing fingers seized around her ankles.

***

Katie climbed through the bare trees on the far side of the lake, arranging her clothes. Taking careful steps through deep snow, she emerged onto the sidewalk and crossed the street toward the stone skyscraper where she worked, stepping inside, smiling at coworkers.

***

"The body of a young woman was found in Lake Melliza today, dressed for winter weather—it's been estimated the body fell through the thin ice of the lake almost six months ago. Due to the time spent underwater, investigators are unsure of the body's identity. There have been no missing persons reports from the area for more than a year, leaving authorities stumped."

If the Holy Grail Were a Person – Eliza Scudder (she/her)

January 1st, 2024

    Last night, had a vision of snakes moving through my body.

January 2nd, 2024

    I remember in seventh grade a teacher I didn't like bullied one of the other students for not having the correct school supplies. The teacher was upset that the cover was broken off the student's binder. I went up to the teacher and asked if I could use the scissors on his desk to cut the cover off my binder. I was looking at him in a way that was sexual when I said that. I think that I was implying that I could slice off his dick. I wasn't really conscious of the meaning of what I was saying.

January 3rd, 2024

    I think it was the summer after seventh grade that my family went to the beach. On the way to the beach I said, "I want to be fancy at the beach." I think that my dad was turned on by what I was saying, and that made my mom feel insecure. My mom insisted that we stop at a fancy restaurant even though no one was hungry. When we were at the fancy restaurant, she said that she was the "breadwinner of the family," so she, "can't be loose."

    I feel like when she calls people loose, she is saying that they could be violently raped.

    I think that a lot of my subconscious beliefs surrounding money stem from my mom calling women loose for not having as much money as her, or for being younger than her, or not having the same job title as her.

    When we got to the beach, I went in the water with my older sister. My dad was staring at me in a way that made me feel like he was thinking about doing violent things to me. I got the sense that my mom said, "Do you think she'll be loose by the time she's Maggie's age?" Maggie is my older sister. I think my mom said violent things about me to turn my dad on. She thinks that calling me loose means she "has a way with words."

January 4th, 2024

Freshman year of high school, I told Casey that I wanted to pretend he was my dad in a way that sounded sexual. Later that year, I asked Casey if he had wide feet. I said I wanted to marry someone with wide feet. Eventually, I became conscious of the meaning of what I was saying.

I said, "Oh no! I don't know what to do." I was very embarrassed. Casey said to talk about The Bible. I said I forgot what was in The Bible. He said, "Thou shalt not covet thy neighbor's wife."

January 5th, 2024

Last October, there was an eclipse. During that eclipse, I had visions of my dad's oldest brother doing sexual things to me as a baby.

January 6th, 2024

It was difficult for me to grow up around my dad. He had a rare, early-onset form of dementia.

January 7th, 2024

Sophomore year of high school, I asked Casey to be my boyfriend.

I think that his dad told him that he could get me to give him a blowjob and get away with it because my family is from Arkansas and Casey's middle name is William. Casey punched his dad in the face for saying that.

My older sister bullied me into breaking up with him because she said that wanting to be in a relationship with someone the same age as me was "trying to fuck a fetus."

She put a bumper sticker on her car that read, "I miss Bill." She was a senior in high school that year. She thought that I would be driving the car after she went off to college. I think she wanted to force me to give people blowjobs because she was mad at me for being a smaller size than her.

My dad ordered the bumper sticker online using my mom's debit card because he didn't have a job. He wanted to be a "stay-at-home dad."

I think he heard that there were other girls my age who gave their boyfriends bow jobs so he thought that I should have to do that too. I think that my dad wanted to harm me.

January 8th, 2024

That same year, my older sister tried to get me to sleep with someone else's boyfriend. She was mad that this girl was a smaller size than her, so she wanted me to steal this girl's boyfriend to bother her. I had never had sex before. I think my older sister treated me like I was her property because she was insecure about no one finding her attractive.

January 9th, 2024

I got my driver's license late. My dad said sexual things to me in the car and was aggressive to me when I tried to get away from him. I didn't like being around my dad, but I think on a subconscious level, I knew I was keeping him away from the younger girls by spending time with him. I feel like my dad was grooming me to have a sexual relationship with him.

January 10th, 2024

I want to go back and talk to my high school teachers. I think a lot of them were really worried about me when I was in high school.

January 11th, 2024

When I was a junior in high school, my mom said to my high school art teacher, "I could be writing Wendell Berry," except she said the word "writing" in a way that sounded like "riding." Wendell Berry is an author from rural Kentucky. I guess my mom was saying that my father was like Wendell Berry because my parents are from the South. I don't know who in their right mind would consent to sex with my father.

Later that day, I was at home trying to do my homework. My mom told me that she could be "writing Wendell Berry." I thought it meant she was going to duct tape a book to a bicycle and ride the bicycle. My dad was in the room. I think she was trying to flirt with him and also trying to make me uncomfortable. She was upset that I didn't understand the hidden meaning of what she was saying. She wanted me to be more sexual than her so that she could call me "loose." I'm surprised no one called child protective services on my parents.

A few months later, my dad told me to go in the bathroom and look in the toilet. He asked if I knew what was in the toilet. I said no. He told me to smell it, and I said I didn't want to. He said it was cum. He said he didn't cum in his pants. I didn't understand the meaning of what he was saying. He was looking at me like I was stupid. He told me to go into the garage. He handed me duct tape and told me to strap my mom's book to her bicycle. He said that we could do it in my younger brother's bed and my mom would never find out. I still didn't understand what he was saying. He was laughing at me and treating me like I was stupid.

January 12th, 2024

    I wanted to run away from home and become a professional mermaid.

    In my early twenties, I told my mom about my plan to run away from home. She said I wouldn't have gotten very far. I think I would have made my way to New York.

January 13th, 2024

    I keep having thoughts of Casey. I feel like I become more creative when I'm connected to his energy.

January 14th, 2024

    Senior year of high school, my dad asked me if the girls my age read Fifty Shades of Grey. It made me really uncomfortable that he said that.

January 15th, 2024

    I remember riding my bike over the summer after I graduated from high school. My mom was mad at me for riding my bike. She said that she never looked the way I looked.

    People at church had told her to go to yoga to keep my dad happy so that he wouldn't be looking at me. She told me that if I was riding my bike, I should have to keep my dad happy, and she wasn't even going to go to yoga anymore. I didn't understand why it mattered whether or not my dad was happy.

January 16th, 2024

    I think that when I was in college, my dad masturbated into the toilet at a restaurant in the town I grew up in. He told the waitress the bathroom needed to be cleaned and said that when I came home from college I could "eat his ice cream."

January 17th, 2024

When I came home after my first semester of college, my dad asked me if the other students at school called me "Lucy." I said that no one had ever called me "Lucy."

January 18th, 2024

I get the sense that my dad was trying to force me into prostitution.

January 19th, 2024

I want to watch the movie *A Haunting in Connecticut*. Someone told me once that it was written about my family. I think there were people who wanted to murder my younger brother to get back at my parents for harming me when I was a child. I think that's what the movie *A Haunting in Connecticut* is about.

January 20th, 2024

Black Moon Lilith is an astrological point named after Adam's first wife. Lilith refused to submit to Adam and was cast out of the Garden of Eden. Black Moon Lilith represents absence, removal, and the potential for creation.

January 21st, 2024

I think that I knew Casey in a past life.

When I see my past life, I am in a garden, sort of like The Secret Garden or The Garden of Eden. I think I was held captive by Nazis. I think they kidnapped me when I was seven and then forced me to become a prostitute by the time I was thirteen. I wore a corset, a push up bra, and a white dress. I was required to always be sexually available. I had everything I needed, and everyone thought I was the prettiest, but I wasn't allowed to leave the garden. I wasn't allowed to say no to anyone. The garden was on the edge of the city and was surrounded by stone walls. Casey was a soldier from another place. He had a gun and brought me outside the city walls. I didn't choose to go with him, but I was safer with him than with the Nazis because when I was with Casey, I only had to have sex with him instead of having to have sex with a lot of people.

I got the sense that the year was 1949 when Casey brought me outside the city walls. I think that the people who held me captive spoke French and Casey spoke Spanish. I didn't speak either of the languages. I think I was born in the Netherlands and maybe had English or German ancestry. I wonder what happened in France in 1949. I know that was after the end of WWII, but for some reason I was still held in captivity until 1949 when Casey rescued me. I think we lived in the woods, somewhere just outside the city, and I made art to sell to tourists.

January 22nd, 2024

Sometimes, I feel like my left arm is detached from my body.

January 23rd, 2024

The planet Jupiter will be conjunct the planet Uranus in the astrological sign of Taurus on April 20th, 2024. When planets are conjunct each other, it means their energies are working together. This will be the most significant astrological occurrence this year. The last time Jupiter was conjunct Uranus in Taurus was at the beginning of WWII.

I had a dream that Casey told me his birthday was April 20th. In my dream, he said that he was born on Gnome Sunday, like Easter Sunday except a celebration of gnomes. I told him about my dream over the phone, and he said his actual birthday was April 30th. He told me that Hitler was born on April 20th and died on April 30th.

January 24th, 2024

    I think my parents are the Antichrist, and I think that I'm the Holy Grail.

January 25th, 2024

    I think that if the Holy Grail were a person, she would pretend to be a prostitute so people wouldn't try to force her into prostitution.

January 26th, 2024

    Last night, I dreamed that some people I didn't know threw me a birthday party. They thought it was my fifteenth birthday even though I told them I would be thirty in June.

    There were some very tall men who said I had to give them my phone before I left the party. I gave them my phone because I was afraid not to. After I left the party, I told someone about leaving my phone there, and he said I should go and ask for it back. We went back to the party, and I asked for my phone back and one of the tall men said I had to go in the other room with him. I asked if he was going to hit me, and he said yes. I ran away and ran all the way to a police station.

    All of the people who were at the party showed up at the police station. They all gave the police their opinion about what happened to my phone.

    Eventually, two extremely tall people, who were both about double the height of a normal human, walked into the police station. They were surrounded by glowing light. Everyone hid their faces and laid on the floor when they walked in. The person next to me laid on top of me to protect me. It was like everyone knew there could be a shooting. The person who laid on top of me to protect me had some sort of device he could use to look around the room without looking up. The device showed that everyone had been removed from the room and my phone was next to me. I was able to walk out of the police station and find my car.

I was about to get in my car when a guy walked up to me and said there were protests at the police station.

He said that some of the older people in the community wanted to talk to me. They wanted me to be safe and free because I'm special, but they wanted me to know that not everyone could be safe and free because not everyone is special.

I went back to the police station, and one of the older women who had been protesting at the station gave me three pendants. The first pendant was like a tree and a brain combined. The second pendant symbolized time, and the third pendant was something to remember her by. She wanted me to wear the pendants on a necklace, so people knew I was special and meant to be protected.

Move Right Through – Rebecca (Becks) Carlyle (she/her)

Aisha couldn't remember how she got here. All she knew was the inky night sky, clouds blotting out light from the stars, and the all-too-present silence. She patted the ground around her with outstretched palms, searching for her glasses on damp dirt, stirring a moist, earthen scent that filled her nostrils. The absence of them pressing down her nose was stark and worrisome. Although Aisha wasn't blind without them, everything would be a little fuzzy around the edges. With eyes squinted, she took in her surroundings, still patting the wet soil to no avail. A big sigh slowly pulled itself from her chest once she had successfully felt her within-reach-radius and hadn't yet bumped into them. She would need to buy another pair of glasses. Again.

It was too quiet here, and that put her on edge. The roadway couldn't be near since she didn't hear any vehicles passing by. She also hadn't felt any grass or gravel when she had been feeling around for her glasses, so Merrim Lake or Twin Pine Park were out. Where else would be this far away from the road?

A sense of dread began to pool deep in her core, spreading quickly through her body, leaving goose-pricked flesh in its wake. She prayed she was wrong. She let the dread drag her from a seated position to standing. With breath coming in unsteady gasps, she took a step forward, squinting into the expansive darkness. She was able to pick out lumps sticking up from the ground every couple of feet in every direction. Some seemed to be rounded, some appeared to have sharp edges, and some had statuesque shapes towering above her short stature. Her right hand reached up instinctively to push glasses back up her nose. Aisha muttered to herself to stop being stupid and strained her eyes harder to see more details. There were trees lining the far left and right, but nowhere in between. Bushes and ivy crawled over each slab in the ground and wove themselves along the pathways in between. She knew without a doubt where she was. The old ranching cemetery.

Now for the real question: how did she get here?

A breeze rattled banyan tree limbs and blew her curly hair away from her face. The air was brisk and startlingly cold on her bare arms. As Aisha folded her arms across her chest to keep her torso warm, another realization hit her. Her jacket was nowhere to be found, which is where her keys and phone would've been. All of her must-have belongings were seemingly missing. Unsure if she was headed in the right direction Aisha took a few steps forward, hoping that the main wrought iron gate was straight ahead. She needed to get home. But mostly, she needed to get out of here. Caution and worry and the loss of her glasses made her progress forward painstakingly slow. Aisha's feet slid ahead, scared to lift them up and trip over something she couldn't see, like the vines and ivy that grew over everything.

The clouds were shifting noticeably, beams of moonlight shooting through and highlighting tombstones for just a moment before falling dark again. She felt as if she were underwater with the filtered light, the audible silence, and the inability to move quickly. Try as she might, Aisha couldn't help but step on a few graves. Her stomach flipped over for disrespecting the dead in this way, but she couldn't see where their edges lay, not with her eyesight in this fuzzy state.

Another breeze swept by, pushing the clouds in front of the moon to the side. Relief flooded through her as light descended on the landscape, but it quickly fled her system and was replaced with fear. Her internal sense of direction had led her in the wrong direction. Directly before her was a mausoleum instead of the gate away from this place. She had been trudging in the wrong direction this entire time. Dismay began to seep its way through her extremities, freezing the blood in her veins. Aisha turned toward where she had been sitting earlier when she came to and squinted to make out the details in the shadows. She couldn't recall there being a mausoleum in the old ranching cemetery, but then again, she wasn't 100% certain that's where she was.

A low-hanging mist weaved its way through the tombstones, sending tendrils forward and inching its way closer to her. It rose into the air, swirling in on itself and creating humanlike shapes above each gravesite. They swayed as one, these ethereal beings gliding just above the ground. A glow outlined each figure, pulsing within them as if it were their life source: *bum-bum... bum-bum...*

She rubbed her eyes—this couldn't be real. Yet when she opened her eyes again, there they were. Without any facial features, they seemed to track her, pulling her closer without ever reaching out an arm or hand. She took a step back, letting the fear get the better of her. Her breath came in uneasy spurts, bursting from her chest and gulping in the night air by the mouthful.

Then they were upon her. The first hovered in place directly before her for a moment. Aisha could see right through the milky film of it, the translucent form wavering under her gaze. As if of its own accord, her hand reached out to touch it. She wanted to feel its texture, expecting it to be soft like a cloud and barely there at all. That's all it took for the apparition to move forward and consume her with its entire being. When it collided into her, Aisha was whisked away from her own body, spiraling through the ether to another time and place.

She felt frail and tired. She was in a bed with a patchwork quilt tucked into all her crevices. She raised a hand and noticed it was old, wrinkled with unpainted nails. What the hell was happening? She was alone in the room. It was barely furnished, with just a chest of drawers across from the foot of the bed and a rocking chair in the corner. An afghan was tossed haphazardly over the back of the chair, the yellow yarn the only spot of color in the room. Exhaustion coerced a heavy sigh from her lips, her eyelids drooping lazily and coming to rest. The last thing she felt before being ripped back to the present was loneliness.

Aisha coughed into her manicured hands, sputtering for air. She looked around for the thing that had just passed through her, but it was gone, evaporated into the night. A shiver rolled through her entire body in a giant, convulsive wave, leaving her a frigid, hollowed-out shell. The misty forms writhed in place, all but two.

One was in front, with another slightly behind it, both moving forward—the first sliding its form onto hers—

Aisha hurtled through space again as she was pulled from herself and tossed into what she thought was another's last moment. This time, she wasn't alone. Instead, she was filled with dread and sorrow. The room was a bright, starched white and smelled of disinfectant and death. She was tightly tucked into an old, thin, slightly raised mattress and hooked up to a machine that beeped every few seconds, monitoring her shallow breathing. The bed was surrounded by loved ones, oppressively so. She would not be going peacefully, not with heaving sobs weighing down the air in the room. She felt her esophagus begin to close up and her chest tighten with lungs that refused to fill.

The room with the family dropped away, and she was torn through the ether and into another body, but this body wasn't old and dying. This felt young and vivacious, pulsing with nervous energy. She was cowering in the dark, curled up on the floor, crawling away from a closed-door rimmed with light. Her chest rose and fell in quick, panicked spurts, fear coursing through her veins— thudding deep in her bones.

From the other side, footsteps clambered by as terror leaped into her mouth, a strangled sound that couldn't come out. They passed by and faded away. She released a lung full of air that she had been holding. The door ripped from its hinges, and the closet flooded with light. A man's silhouette towered over her, a kitchen knife held at his side, dripping with red. The scream she had been repressing clawed up her throat right as she was torn back into herself once more.

Aisha stood in the graveyard, shaking and wailing. She didn't want to look up, didn't want to see how many of these she would have to go through before she'd arrive at the fence line. There had to be another way out of the graveyard, a way around where she didn't have to see and feel these people's final moments. She swiveled her head from one side of the yard to the other, squinting through her blurred vision to make out the walkways and fence line.

If there were any breaks in the fence, they weren't visible. Unsure of which direction to go, panic settled in. Another misty, featureless figure was almost upon her now. Her feet began to move, scrambling underneath herself before her brain could catch up with them, but she wasn't quick enough to outmaneuver the ghost.

This one moved through her almost too fast to register. A sense of foreboding flooded her senses, swept her from where she stood, hurtling her up two marble steps and into a wall. Panic and confusion prickled her cold flesh, a shiver rippling up through her spine. Flashes of sharp steel and the steady drip of warm blood hovered in her gaze. A jolt of pain seared into her stomach, ripping another painful shriek from her frame. The back of her skull smacked the wall behind her, and everything vanished; she was herself once more.

With her own senses returned, Aisha scrambled and tried to escape from the shifting films. Instinct told her to go inside the building she found herself outside. The glass door was tall and heavier than it appeared. Her hands searched for a handle or knob before pushing with her full weight in order to budge the door enough to slip inside and away from the ectoplasmic beings that chased her. She hoped they couldn't pass through the walls and doors as they passed through her, that she was safe in this building.

Cold oozed from the walls, roiling through the room in the wind, twisting, turning, and expelling its musty air on her. She moved to the middle of the room and let her eyes rove about it, exploring all the nooks and crannies. Aisha couldn't see much of the ceiling or if there were lights anywhere, not with her subpar vision. She reached out a hand and let it drag across the wall, guiding her through the room. The wall seemed to have boxes etched in it, her fingers lingering on what she assumed were name plaques. A horrific realization entered her mind: she was in a mausoleum. As if summoned by the idea of them, wisps of white began to seep into the air, escaping through the cracks of their forever homes and rising to greet her.

The first of this group made her old and frail; like her bones were about to splinter into a million pieces within her skin. She fell down a flight of stairs, tripping over her nonslip, orthopedic sneaker-clad feet. She felt a rib crack and give way, a knee pop in the wrong direction, a gash on her shoulder, and finally, her head smacking the wooden floor. She lay there, the minutes ticking by and no one coming to help her, her vision coming and going in time with her fading pulse.

She came to on the floor of the mausoleum, relieved that her own strong bones were holding her up, still poised by the door. She tried the handle and pushed, then pulled. It wouldn't budge; it remained steadfast and immovable. Immobilized by terror, Aisha was locked inside with a room full of spirits. Her chin wobbled with her emotions, and she looked up just in time to see two mists coming for her. They both reached her at the same time, fighting for their own stories to be heard.

Her head pounded, and she was startled by the sensation of someone's hands squeezing around her neck—

She was in a luxurious bed with fluffy comforters pulled about her and pillows propped behind her head—

She was trying to fight back, clawing at her attacker's face—

Beside her on the bedside table was an empty pill bottle, and her stomach roiled with putrid heat—

She felt her knees giving way as her strength began to fade, her throat rasping for air, high-pitched ringing in the depths of her ears. Her fingernails cut slashes across his face, red filling her vision—

Her heart rate was slowing, she could tell. She was cold, pulling the sheets and blankets tighter about herself. Her mind bounced from one thing to the next, unable to focus itself. Her chest tightened, and she gasped her last breath—

Aisha was sitting on the floor when the two mists left her exhausted body. They had fought hard to show her their individual deaths. With her energy drained from the exertion of being pulled back and forth between the two, she couldn't move. Her limbs wouldn't obey the command to stand up and get out. She stayed on the ground and waited for the next wave to hit.

Bluebells – Rebecca (Becks) Carlyle (she/her)

A dense fog blanketed the low valleys, hiding the river banks that cut through the sprawling land. It was a still dawn, and the slowly rising sun struggled to shine through. She stood on the terrace with a navy, wool coat draped over her shoulders and worn walking boots, keeping her toes safe from the crisp air.

She realized she was still clutching the now cold cup of Assam. She had steeped it hours before, after giving up the farce—sleep wasn't coming for her. She couldn't remember the last time she dreamed. Without sleep, one doesn't dream, and she was too busy to spend her days with wishful thinking.

A deep sigh escaped her; she felt her lungs deplete and empty. Susanah, her cousin, would admonish her when she found her awake before the staff once again. She turned from the milky sight and went inside, closing the double patio doors behind her and letting the heavy brocade drapings block the light. The room was dark, but she knew the way. She let her fingertips glide along shelf after shelf of book spines. This was her favorite room in Susanah's estate. The library was a safe space, a place to rest, recharge, and gather herself. A place to breathe in history, art, and philosophy. Thankfully, after everything she'd been through, her cousin left her to her own devices when she retreated here.

Pausing briefly at the end of the room, she picked up and relighted her gas lantern. The room glowed a familiar auburn, although the flame still sparked a passing moment of terror in her core. The golden flicker invoked an image of the city alight, smoke blotting out the sky, and an acrid smell burning her nostrils. She shuttered, shaking off the memory.

She took the lantern with her through the manor's halls, an orb of light illuminating her path to the kitchen once more. She poured out her cold tea and began the process again, placing the kettle on the stovetop and adding tea leaves to the strainer. She carried her cup to the little wooden table in the corner and took a seat where she could keep an eye on the kettle.

Absentmindedly, she spun the simple gold band on her left ring finger. She still hadn't conjured the courage to take it off yet. It didn't feel right, but then, she didn't think it ever would. How was she supposed to move forward while he was pushing up daisies? Shocked at her own thoughts, she spun the ring faster. She wondered if their initials would ingrain themselves into her skin if she never took it off.

Mrs. Fletcher came puttering in just then, lighting the room and rendering the lantern useless.

"I thought I might find you here, dear."

"Good morning, Mrs. Fletcher. You're up early today." She folded her hands in her lap.

"I was hoping to have your mornin' tea ready for you, but alas, you've woken before me again."

She didn't bother correcting Mrs. Fletcher. She hadn't woken early; she merely hadn't gone to sleep at all. Oh, she'd tried. She had lain in bed every night, as she always did, staring at the thick canopied four-poster above her. The burgundy felt oppressive, as if she were staring at the lining of a coffin. She tried closing her eyes, but only for a moment. The dark took frightful shapes of tumbling brick buildings crumbling from the insides. Cobblestoned streets cracked and split, creating jutting cliffs. Her eyes would flick back open at this point, clearing the vision.

The kettle whistled briefly before Mrs. Fletcher plucked it up and filled her cup. The steam warmed her face, and she breathed in the earthy aroma while listening to the middle-aged woman bustle about the room, preparing for the day.

Taking her fresh cup with her, she stood and bid the housekeeper farewell, promising to attempt to get some rest. She pattered down the marble hallways aimlessly, floating steam marking her path. She passed through the grand foyer, through the east sitting room, to the music room, and into the conservatory. The window seat called to her, as it did every morning. She seated herself on the plush velvet cushion with a stack of pillows propped behind her. The Austen book she had tossed aside yesterday remained where she had left it. Sometimes, she felt like she had landed at Pemberly itself, although not quite as happily as Lizzie Bennet had.

She loved this view. She had never loved the tight buildings and crowded alleyways of San Francisco, to look outside and only see identical building after building. Technically, it should've been her home—she was born and raised there as her parents had moved to America shortly after they married and before she was born. Yet, she never felt at home. Here, though, this was where she belonged.

It was then that Susanah swept into the room. She was an enigmatic woman, drawing attention even when she wasn't trying. Susanah's chestnut locks were already pulled back with ringlets cascading down her back with a bejeweled clip holding them in place. She was still in her dressing gown, but she somehow came off as stylish. The pastel pink complemented her complexion, and the ruffles along the hemlines and belled wrist cuffs accentuated her movements.

"Good morning; I thought I would find you here. Didn't sleep again?" Susanah sat beside her on the window bench, keeping her attention solely on her.

She shook her head, then took a sip of the brown liquid; it was no longer steaming. She wondered how long she had been sitting here observing the peaceful valleys outside, listening to the warblers sing.

"Did you try dabbing rose oil to your neck like I told you to?"

She hadn't. She'd felt too silly. It was just an old family trick that didn't actually work. Like drinking warm milk or ensuring one's sheets were linen. She truly appreciated her cousin but struggled with all these rural beliefs. It was so different from the city life. She had traded America for her English roots and the ruined city for the countryside.

"Of course, I tried it," she fibbed. What harm would it do? Susannah couldn't possibly understand the trauma she'd been through. Durham didn't have earthquakes, not like the California coastline—it's why she'd been so ready to accept her cousin's offer to visit for an extended stay.

Her cousin sighed. "Cecy, are you sure I can't call the family doctor? There must be something we can do. You can't go on like this. You look like you're going to collapse at any moment."

"Susanah, I'm fine. It'll work itself out." She wasn't sure if it was the posh accent, the differing upbringing, or if it was just Susanah, but her tone of condescension made Cecy feel like a child, even though they were the same age.

Concern dotted Susanah's porcelain face. She meant well, but all Cecy wanted was to be left alone. She didn't want to talk about it and relive every moment of the disaster. How could she expect Susanah to understand? Her cousin hadn't lost anyone close to her before nor experienced a natural disaster firsthand. She had grown up here in the secluded wilderness of Durham with a home full of staff waiting for her beck and call.

"There is another option..." Susanah's expression had changed to one of mischief. "Have you heard much about hypnotherapy?"

She'd heard of it in hushed tones before but nothing more. She shook her head, aware that Susanah managed to look poised at an early hour while she looked like her stress personified. Cecy pictured what she must look like to Susanah, clothes disheveled from a restless night, nutmeg hair messily swept atop her head, darkened circles beneath her eyes that no amount of cucumber slices could seem to banish.

"There's a man in town who goes by the name of Doctor Price. I don't know if that's his real name. Anyway, he studied under Jean-Martin Charcot—"

"The man who tried to diagnose hysteria?" Cecy couldn't stop herself from interrupting.

Susanah seemed annoyed by her tone of disbelief, seemingly unaware of how offensive she sounded by proposing such a fraudulent treatment. "Hypnotherapy is still seen as a viable option. At least discreetly."

"What exactly are you suggesting?"

"What if Doctor Price could make you forget all that unpleasant business? You might be able to sleep—move on with your life. I just loath seeing you like this." Susanah placed a gentle hand on Cecy's knee, her eyes imploring her to give it a go.

"This is absurd," she laughed and immediately regretted it. Her cousin retracted her hand and sat up taller, her feelings wounded. "How can you be sure it would even work? It's not a legitimate medical practice."

"Doctor Price is very reputable. I have it on good authority that he cured the little Mason girl of her shakes in four meetings."

Cecy supposed she could always beg off later, but Susanah would be so disappointed. All she wanted to do was help.

"Very well," Cecy agreed.

"Excellent. I'll have Mr. Harris send a message right away. Come along, dear; we have a busy day ahead of us in town. My wedding won't plan itself."

Susanah swept out of the room just as she had arrived, a whirlwind of energy following in her wake. She pondered what hypnosis would feel like—what it would mean to forget the earthquake, the fire, the destruction of everything she had known. Would she forget her parents? Or Russell? She hoped not. However, she wouldn't mind losing the image of pulling brick after brick off their lifeless, debris-covered forms until emergency responders dragged her away from the ruins. She remembered how much her throat burned and scratched; she never learned if it was from the smoke inhalation or the screaming.

Cecy returned her gaze out the window; she didn't feel like going to town with Susanah to look at place settings and table linens. The fog still lingered, but the sun had risen and spread light through the slade, bluebells swaying in the subtle breeze. She would've liked bluebells at her wedding, an intimate ceremony surrounded by the little blue flowers bobbing about her skirts. She'd only heard Susanah talk about gardenias.

CW: drug use, horror-typical gore/violence

Fosrsythia – Justine Witkowski (any pronouns)

Los Angeles. 1992.

By the time I met Forsythia, I'd been awake for thirty-six hours.

Part of it was my own fault. Between a liquid diet of espresso and the occasional break for blow, I was wired. Although neither of these things came into the picture until sleeplessness had long-since crawled up inside me and made its home. They alleviated the exhaustion, but neither was the actual cause. That title was reserved for the inoperable, walnut-sized tumor pressed up against my brain, making sleep fitful at best and nonexistent at worst.

Insomnia was the only real symptom I was experiencing back then—though I would've traded it for just about anything else. On the off chance that I got those three or four hours of sleep in, my dreams were so vivid I began to wonder if it was any different from being awake. Stimulants probably didn't help with this, but without them, I was more or less a walking corpse, so tired that some days, even the sunlight hurt.

There were upsides to all of this, one being that I was always either too high or too tired to reckon with the fact that I'd be dead within a year. The other was that I had more time to draw, and by some miracle, I still had the energy to do it. Before my diagnosis, I worked in billing for a hospital , working just shy of sixty hours a week and mostly processing palliative care bills. You wouldn't believe the amount of people shelling out thousands on the verge of death, be it for radiation, AZT or some other treatment that was killing them faster than any disease could. Chemo was uncomfortable on a bill but seeing it in full swing on the people paying those bills scared the living shit out of me. Pallid, skeletal, and in immense pain for the sake of prolonging the life of a cancerous tit or pancreas, almost always at the insistence of a well-meaning but, nonetheless, out of touch loved one. Unlike them, the only person making my decisions was me, and I'd be damned to hell if was going to spend what was left of my life in that place.

I quit as soon as I had enough proof to file for disability, which more than took care of the few things I needed. Without sleep or work, drawing was my only purpose anyway. The city occasionally caught my interest—details, like the swallowing of a stucco wall by a bougainvillea, the exposed pipes of a fountain, a bloated Queen palm—although people were always the preference. I produced hundreds of sketches of people I'd never met or spoken to. Waiting for the bus, picking up hookers, mowing their lawns, kissing, sleeping, fighting—you name it. It was easy to slip into the pattern, passing longer and longer stretches of time in transience.

Day and night were slowly losing their meanings. There were times I was on my third or fourth attempt at a nightcap while the sun began its hazy, bleeding ascent above the smog. I sat in patches of grass in nothing but two-day-old tank tops and sweatpants, watching 9-5 commuters shuffle down the sidewalks and into city buses or company cars. Even the whores and hustlers knew when it was time to go home. Neon twenty-four-hour signage was programmed to turn on and off. Solar panels knew when to collect and when to provide. Morning glories opened and shut. I existed outside all of them, trapping little pieces of their souls in graphite and ink while they remained none the wiser.

I could've kept going this way until I died. It wasn't a bad way to spend what remained of twenty-seven otherwise wasted years. I might've found peace this way. I might've been content.

Thanks to Forsythia, I'll never know for sure

I didn't give her much thought the first few times I saw her. She'd been crawling the Lost Dawn for a while, the same less-than-covert lesbian dive I frequented for worthwhile subjects and occasional tail. The place had grown pretty lonely in the past few months. HIV was the most likely reason. Out of those I knew who'd contracted it, not one had been a woman, but I supposed you could never be too cautious. Rapists and queer bashers liked easier targets—almost always the reason for the missing person posters that would sporadically emerge amidst the sea of sticky fliers beside the door. There'd been more of them recently, and the part that always got to me was that they were never official. Instead, it was always a piece of copy paper with a photo printed or pasted across the front, the name and information scrawled across the top in sharpie by some distraught friend, lover, or, if nothing else, a community member choosing to give a fuck when LAPD didn't. In a lot of ways, Lost Dawn was a constant reminder of how bad things had gotten, as if people didn't get enough of that everywhere else. I couldn't blame them for staying away. I probably wouldn't have done much different if I thought I had enough time left for it to make a difference.

The girls that still showed up in spite of everything seemed to avoid Forsythia like the plague. It was odd, considering she wasn't exactly bad looking. She wasn't a super model or anything, but she had a sort of delicate, doll-like prettiness about her, with big blue eyes, an androgyne face, and carefully blown out and straightened blond hair that hung around it. I figured no one wanted much to do with her since she also had the look of every other clubby bitch slumming out of Bel Air or Malibu, but knowing what I do now, I wonder if everyone else simply sensed something I didn't.

It might've been the reason why she ended up desperate enough to approach me.

"I see you here a lot," she said, sliding into a chair across from me "Are you some kind of artist? Or just a pervert?" It sounded like a joke, but her face didn't change, staring at me, expectant and wide-eyed.

"An artist, hopefully," I scoffed, deciding to throw her a bone. "What about you? You like looking for perverts?"

"Not particularly." she said, shifting her gaze to my closed sketchbook. "You draw then?"

"It would seem like that, yeah."

"Would I know your name from a gallery or anything like that?"

"Probably not," I said, "but if you're interested, it's Julie. What about you?"

"Forsythia." she replied absently. "Can I see your drawings, Julie?"

I placed a hand over the glossy black cover, suddenly feeling protective. "Hm, I don't know. How about you buy me a drink first?"

"Sure." She tapped the rim of my empty glass with a long, manicured fingernail. "Jack and Coke, right?"

I blinked. "Yeah. Uh, were you watching me or something?"

"I could smell the residue," she said plainly, already standing up. "Be right back."

"Wait." There was no way I was letting her leave off on that. "You could...*smell it?*"

"I have an above average sense of smell."

"What, you sniff out bombs too?"

She shrugged.

"Forget the drink." I decided. I was on my fourth anyway and was starting to enter that unpleasant territory of tiredness that came with drinking. If I was going to keep up with her, I needed a second wind. "I don't like watching people go through my stuff, so I'm gonna run to the restroom if you want to look through it while I'm gone."

"Are you sure—"

"Yeah," I replied, barely sticking around long enough for her to sit back down. "Go crazy. But don't take it anywhere either. I'll be right back."

As soon as I stood up, I realized I was drunker than I thought, trying to keep my balance between tables and tattered barstools. One benefit of Lost Dawn's denial of its emptiness was the ample amount of seating it still had to brace for a fall. It was good for me, at least, given that I hadn't been upright since I got there, and wasn't sure if I was actually falling forward or if it just felt that way.

As I careened in the direction of the bathrooms, more posters of missing girls took the places of Sports Illustrated hard bodies and the occasional cracked, faded beer signage. They were like shadows, relegated to the darker, less traveled corners, like that had to be the compromise if they wanted to be seen at all. Out of sight and out of mind except for the brief spurt of time you spend taking a piss. Part of me always felt like I'd end up there some day.

The bathroom wasn't near as thought provoking, unless you could be moved by toilet poetry and the occasional variation on "so-and-so is a cheating snatch". With three white stalls and alternating cream and pale pink tiles lining the walls, it was practically asking to be vandalized. The only exception and, coincidentally, my favorite thing about it, were the stainless-steel feminine products trash cans affixed to each stall. I was sure they were an inconvenience to most people, being so close that your knees knocked up against them when you sat down, but the lid was just wide and flat enough to cut a line on.

Unfortunate for me, the teener in my pocket wasn't even close to being as full as I remembered, hardly containing enough for even the skinniest of lines. It certainly wasn't worth the hassle of fucking with a card and straw, so I went ahead and dug my pinky finger into the bag, snorting whatever I could scrape beneath my nail.

At some point between the burn and numbing of my nose, I was out. Heart hammering in perfect sync with each quick stride up to the grime-smeared mirror, so I thought I could still hear my footsteps as I stood still taking in my reflection. Each strand of lank black hair on my head seemed to catch light in its own way while the delicate red veins snaking over the whites of my eyes made the irises appear darker and sharper. I still looked beyond tired, but the dark ridges and valleys of my face felt right, melding into a complex geography of bruises, moles and hollow circles stretched tight over every protruding bone. Thousands of tiny live wires pulsed beneath my skin, and it was the only form fit to contain them.

I was fucking electric.

When I came back, Forsythia was still examining each page with a look of serious deliberation on her face, unbothered by the whir and chatter of the bar. She kept this up until she reached the middle, turning the book back around to face me and tapping the page, "What's this?"

I craned my neck forward only for a pang of embarrassment to shoot through me. It was one of the less tasteful drawings, a woman reaching up to wipe a bead of sweat from her neck. I wasn't sure exactly when or why I'd drawn it, only that I'd been sick, delirious and coming off a bender, having taken the personal liberty of using that position to draw her topless and fervently scratching at her chest. Muted gray tones of blood and skin marked the space between her breasts and navel, contrasting sourly with shadows scratched on with a dying pen. "Sorry," I said weakly, "I was just, uh—I wasn't thinking straight and just wanted to try something. I don't know where it came from."

Forsythia persisted, unshaken. "Were you working from imagination?"

I tried to think of something clever to say, only to come back with, "Well…duh."

"Do you work better from sight?" Not up to her standards, then.

"Most people work better that way." I explained, trying not to feel wounded "And you know, there's not exactly a surplus of women out and about scratching themselves 'til they bleed."

For the first time since we started talking, a smile played at her lips, something I couldn't help but feel proud playing a part in. "If you're looking for compelling subjects, I could help you."

"Yeah, on what terms?"

"I can show you something you've never seen before by nine tomorrow night. My only terms are that I get to see whatever you end up drawing." She suddenly looked shy. "I'm staying at the Holiday Inn across the street. Room fifty-four."

Everything about Forsythia fascinated me. Her physical grace seemed to contradict her awkward mannerisms, yet this didn't make her any less intoxicating. On the contrary, it made it hard to get enough of her. Odd ones had always been a favorite of mine, and she was about as odd as they came. Even if she hadn't made that offer, it still wouldn't have taken much to win me over. Hell, I would've asked to go home with her right then and there if she hadn't made the first move. If tomorrow was what she wanted, though, I could wait.

"Room fifty-four," I repeated, feeling myself smiling back at her. "You'll have to write it down for me, but it sounds like a date."

The next night came early for me. After leaving the Lost Dawn, I didn't crash and burn until two the next afternoon. When I woke up again, the sun had just set, and I could hear the soft cries of mourning doves settling in for the night. They were the only constant left in my life, never wavering in their sad, throaty sounds. If I could hear them, I could pretend I was somewhere quieter, waking from an eight-hour sleep to sunlight and sprinklers.

It was always a peaceful first few minutes before reacclimating myself to my apartment, which had never been clean to begin with, but was steadily making the transition from clutter to filth. My sheets were fermented with three months of sweat, stains, and burn holes, smelling vaguely of my body and whatever food I'd eaten there. I had what some people called a "kitchenette" that didn't contain much beyond a stove and enough room on the counter for a hot plate, so when I was feeling okay enough to keep something down, I usually ate in bed. The dishes from those meals sat primarily on one end of the floor while my dirty clothes sat on the other, with both sides having, no doubt, developed thriving ecosystems. There were seeds and stems mashed into the carpet from when I still smoked pot, and I often wondered when they would join forces to finally turn the place into a superfund site.

Mold. Sweat. Pot. Rot. Needless to say, the mourning doves were a good morale booster.

It was a mix between denial and fantasy that consoled me enough to get out of bed most days. This time, however, I had Forsythia to think about. From the second I woke up to when I made it to her door, I considered what was waiting for me. A cynical part of me worried it was just going be her waiting for me completely nude, like she thought I was some sort of romantic still-life artist. I knew I would lose any attraction to her if that were the case and hoped instead that she had something truly unique in store, that she possessed the depth and ingenuity I believed her to be capable of.

***

You can only imagine how I felt when she showed me the woman—naked, gagged, and tied to the bedposts.

There was only the one bed in the room, one Forsythia had presumably slept in before that night. A portable cassette player sat on the nightstand, cranking out the grainy, blown-out sounds of "For Your Eyes Only" by Sheena Easton , as if this was all supposed to be oh-so-sentimental. A plastic shower liner had been pulled over the pristine white sheets beneath her and it looked as if she'd been there long enough that the heat of her body caused patches of condensation to form between the folds, the moisture glistening in the soft glow of the lamp. Save for the shallow rise and fall of her chest, she was perfectly still.

I drew in a sharp breath. "What the fuck—"

"Don't be angry," she said quickly. "I promise, it'll be worth your while."

"I don't draw porn," I snapped. "Not even the rough stuff. Like I said at the bar, I'm not some kind of fucking pervert!"

She looked surprised for a moment, as if only just realizing how this must've looked, before muttering, "It's not porn."

"Yeah, then what the hell is it?"

"Please, Julie, just sit down and—"

"No, no, quit talking to me like you know me." I grabbed her by her shoulders, holding her so tightly I could almost feel bruises blooming beneath my fingertips. "What are you going to do?"

"I'm going to kill her."

Something dropped and twisted in my stomach. I let go of her.

"But you have to see it," she went on, "I've seen work from dozens—hundreds—of other artists over the years and yours was the only one that ever came close to being able to capture this. The gestures, the expressions, the marks—it has to be you."

"Why?" My voice sounded tiny and weak, swallowed by disbelief and the whir of the window unit. "Why do it like—no, why do it at all?"

"I—" she closed her eyes for a second and took a deep breath before opening them again. "Where did you grow up, Julie?"

I let myself sink down onto the edge of the bed, careful not to touch the woman beside me.

"LA." I sniffed "I never left, but—"

"Then maybe you'll understand what it means to keep something with you." she said "I grew up in the Ozarks. My father was a meat processor, nothing grand, nothing terrible, but he took the time and taught all four of my brothers. It wasn't my place to learn. To teach me was beneath him. *I* was beneath him. Do you think I felt slighted by that? Do you think I grew resentful?"

"I—I don't know. . .probably?" I swallowed hard. "I mean, I would."

"No." she said, so quiet I could barely hear her. "I knew early on that there were better things waiting for me. They could never feel or smell things the way I did, as strongly. No one could, so why would I hold myself to their standards? Why would I long to settle for a cold, rotten carcass that doesn't even belong to me?

It's only like this that I get to reap a warmth and pleasure they'll never know. And only you can make it immortal."

A few things occurred to me then. The first and most obvious was that this wasn't all there was to it, that a little bit of sexism couldn't have been the lone catalyst for murder, not that I knew what it might've been otherwise. The next thing—the way people kept their distance from her, the missing posters at the Lost Dawn—all of it made me wonder how many of those disappearances she was responsible for. I could've been in just as much danger as the woman strapped to the bed, although for some reason, she was bound, gagged, and nude while I was not. Despite the utter insanity of it all, I couldn't help but feel special, like the favored worshipper of an otherwise cruel and indifferent god. After being alone for so long, it felt good to be looked at like that. It felt good to be the exception.

"Why, then?" I asked finally. "There are hundreds of other artists in LA. All more talented, more accomplished, more...stable, I guess. Why me?"

Forsythia's expression softened, and when she spoke, she almost sounded sympathetic. "I could smell you dying. I smelled it as soon as I saw you. I couldn't squander it. I needed you."

It was like someone knocked the wind out of me. All the pain and exhaustion, replaced by anticipation until now, came rushing back. I needed to lie down. I needed a cigarette. I needed to throw up. I needed to do a line. I needed to get the fuck out of there.

I needed a lot of things at that moment, but more than anything I needed, I wanted Forsythia. I should've been repulsed and outraged at how sick and selfish this was, but I wasn't. I couldn't help but fantasize about how good it would feel to get that sort of likeness on the page, arched atop a gored form like some sort of angel. How good it would feel for her to want it just as badly, to want something only I could provide. Even if it had to be like this.

It would be just this once, I told myself, easily swaying disgust to compliance. Something truly invigorating, beyond morals, ethics or logic. Just once, before I died. Like I had for every day of my life before this encounter, I tried to convince myself I'd be content with that. That I could stop myself, that it was somehow going to be enough for me. Me, with my endless appetites for drugs, with an instinctive gravitation toward a violence that was never there, with my cancer-ridden brain, slowly catching fire with a disease as insatiable as its host.

I sighed and began patting down my pockets for a stick of graphite.

Forsythia smiled—a real one this time, one that deepened the corners of her mouth and danced across her eyes. If it wasn't over for me already, it was then, as I allowed her to guide me to the wicker chair that sat at the foot of the bed. She rifled through my bag for a second, tossing out prescription bottles, flash drives and a tube of Chapstick before finding my sketchbook and placing it in my lap.

"How are you gonna do it?" I asked. "And why isn't she fighting you?"

"Her *name* is Carmen. That's what her driver's license said, anyway. And it's quick release morphine," she replied, pulling the top nightstand drawer open. After a careful process of digging, she unfurled a thick chef's knife roll across the side of the bed. The knives were immaculately clean and freshly sharpened, although the roll itself had grown dark and sticky with oxidized blood. "There should be enough in her system that she won't feel anything when I cut her open. You might want to get something down before I start—"

"Don't tell me what to do," I murmured, half-assing a joke and half-assing trying to regain my composure. "I'm the artist."

"Say less."

She pulled one of the larger knives from the roll, pressing it into Carmen's skin until it gave way to her breastbone, making a slit all the way down to her groin with surgical precision. A few glistening beads of scarlet swelled into pulsing streams over her chest and abdomen. Just as she said, Carmen didn't appear to feel much of anything, only letting out a soft groan whenever the blade knocked a bone or hit a sensitive spot.

Dark, ruby red depressions had already started to pool up in the shower liner before I remembered I was supposed to be drawing this. Despite being the object of mutilation, Carmen's limp form was easy to take down, textures and all. It was Forsythia's that was difficult, constantly strained and twisted as she pulled back the skin and set about gutting her. With the same zeal of a child about to put their hands in a touch tank, Forsythia plunged both hands beneath her rib cage. The look on her face then was one of pure ecstasy, reaching deeper and deeper into Carmen's chest cavity, pulling out more and more, until I could hear the crack of ribs breaking. Forsythia's right arm was in almost to her shoulder when something sinewy and wet tore lose.

Carmen arched forward wildly, followed by the kicking of her unbound legs and a gasping, strangled sound that told me if Forsythia had not just removed some vital part of her throat, she'd be screaming.

The bucking and twisting caused the shower liner to slip, throwing blood over the wall, the lampshades, and across our faces. Despite the abundance of knives, she fumbled for a loose end of the liner, pulling it tight over Carmen's face. She held it there for what felt like an eternity until Carmen stopped thrashing, her lips glistening and blue.

Forsythia's breathing was still panicked and labored, bloody plastic clenched between her fingers, while I had to remind myself to breathe at all. I'd forgotten Carmen was still alive until then and was still reeling from the shock of her movement, of her fear, of pain excruciating enough to pull her from the depths of a morphine-induced sleep. It suddenly felt real again, and as I glanced back down at the page, I saw that blood had found its way there as well, spattering in from the corner of the page and smeared beneath my hand.

When I lifted it, I had the bloody likeness of Forsythia reaching in to tear out esophagus.

I vomited ten minutes later.

I wondered how much it had to do with what I'd seen as opposed to the state my body was in—even before I got sick, it seemed to be my natural response to stress. It felt far more physical than disgust alone, choking, spitting and dry-heaving until there was nothing left inside me, not even spit or bile. It was so forceful, I was afraid I'd pissed myself until I realized my entire body was covered in sweat. I barely had the strength to lift my face from the toilet seat when Forsythia came to check on me, still covered in Carmen's blood.

"I stole a look at your drawing," she said, sitting cross-legged beside me.

I swallowed back a gag as the scent of blood hit my nose.

"It was beautiful."

"Yeah? Good."

She smoothed back my slick, matted hair. "You're beautiful, too." Only someone like Forsythia could look at me pale and puking and say that honestly. "I want to think—I want to believe you understand me. The way you put it all together—there's something genuine there. There must be."

There was so much I wanted to say to her then. So much I wanted to ask her. I decided I didn't have a problem with her being this way, but I had no idea how I was supposed to proceed. I wanted to tell her how sick and tired and in love I felt. How badly, after less than twenty-four hours I wanted to know her—truly know her. All I could do then, however, was let myself fall limply against her, burying my cold, wet face in her neck.

With the pads of her thumbs pressed up against my temples, she pulled me back up and kissed me, her mouth feverishly hot against mine. "Stay with me," she breathed, "for whatever time you've left." She licked at the little spots of puke stuck at corners of my lips. "I'll do anything for you, anything to make it worth your time. Just promise you'll stay."

No one had ever loved me like that. As far as I knew, no one was supposed to love anyone like that. Even if I had another sixty years ahead of me, there was never going to be another chance like this. Never someone as disgusting and devoted.

There was never going to be another Forsythia.

Wild Daughter – Jordan Nishkian (she/her)

In grief, we keep.

By the time Grandma died, her house had become a museum. This morning, when we pulled into the oil-stained carport, Mom hesitated before turning off the ignition. During the four-hour drive it took to get us into the valley, she and I had mostly ridden in comfortable silence, and now, I saw her want for words. The corners of her lips were pensive, tinted with a practical berry lip balm. The new matriarch.

We exchanged looks. I saw the creases under her eyes route themselves into her cheekbones. We were both tired, running off the sheer determination that oldest daughters are born with. The low rumble of her SUV ceased with a large exhale that came from her belly.

"You don't have to say anything right now," I wanted to tell her.

She rubbed my shoulder. "Ready to work?"

I nodded, reminding myself that the house wouldn't smell like Crisco when we walked in. There wouldn't be food waiting for us in the oven. Grandma wouldn't be peeling apple slices over the kitchen counter.

Although orderly, my grandma hoarded memories. Mom and I volunteered for the first, most intensive round of getting the house sorted. I was an archaeologist, she was a Capricorn, we both liked scavenger hunts. I pushed the door open with my shoulder—it always got a little stuck in the summer—while Mom unfolded a piece of paper from her purse.

"I think we can find most of these things by lunchtime," she said, scanning the list she made from Grandma's will. "We can get enchiladas."

We were greeted with stale, still air. Morning light trickled through the gaps in the curtains, but it was enough to capture the movement of particles swimming around us.

"I'll open some windows," I offered, watching the sea of dust part as I broke through it. The sounds of my heels against the linoleum, of the rushing curtains, of the street and the next-door neighbors' pool broke the unsettling quiet.

I reached over the sink to open the kitchen window as my mom opened the sliding glass door on the other side of the breakfast counter. There was a small dish and a paring knife in the basin, and the roll of paper towels would soon need replacing.

"The roses look great," Mom said. We both looked out to the backyard, and if I unfocused my eyes, I could see blurs of a bounce castle, a slip'n'slide, a family reunion dancing circle. Memories of throwing chopped walnuts to the blue jays on the grass, chasing squirrels along the fence, and squishing fallen, soft apricots in between my toes flooded the front of my mind. Now, the lawn was crisp and brown, and the apricot tree hadn't produced fruit in years. Only in the shade of an Oregon Ash, eight rose bushes had reached the peak of their blooms.

"You loved running around barefoot out there," she told me. "The little burrs would stick your feet, but you kept your shoes off anyway."

I smiled and made my way around the counter to turn on the kitchen lights. Mom was still lost outside. "Remember you'd stay here for weeks during the summer?"

"Course."

"You'd be so brown by the time I picked you up. You haven't been that dark in a long time." She rubbed her hand across her pale arm. "I haven't either."

Over years and loss, the rooms had become subtle, inadvertent shrines. There were tracks in the vinyl where my grandpa would drag the legs of his favorite chair. Figurines of angels were perched on the TV stand in front of where my aunt's hospice bed used to be. A shadow box on the wall next to my grandma's bed encased her mother's pearl hairpin (I planned on keeping this; Great-Grandma Sira was my namesake).

I cleared some space on the kitchen table and peeked at the list she was holding. "You're getting Auntie Joy's silverware?"

Mom let out a small laugh. "Everyone gives me their silverware."

"I'm getting a 'large red box and its contents.'"

"Do you know what that means?"

"No. What does it mean?" I asked.

"I don't know. It's very cryptic." She shrugged and opened the china cabinet drawers. "I'm going to start packing these dishes for Rosie if you want to start looking around for the other things."

The first three items on the list: my grandmother's cross pendant (left to Allyse, my younger cousin with a Proverbs tattoo), Grandpa's Bibles with the notes in the margins (left to my Uncle Warren, now a preacher in Hawaii), and Christmas ornaments (left to my mom, whose tree branches bowed heavy with her already-impressive collection).

"You get the ornaments too," I told her.

"I know," she said under the gentle clacking of plates as she wrapped them in old dish towels. "Sometimes I wonder who will take all of mine when I'm gone."

"I will."

She threw me a face. "You're not sentimental."

I thought of the boxes full of photographs and birthday cards that lived under my bed. "I could be."

"Maybe your brother will. He's more traditional anyway."

"Mom, I'll get a tree once I have space for one. I'm not anti-Christmas tree."

"Okay," she dismissed. "If you find more old towels by the bathroom, will you bring them back?"

"Sure."

I headed toward the back of the house where I'd find the Bibles and the necklace. There were three bedrooms: the small pink one with a vintage vanity was my aunt's, the white one with the red '80s stripe around the wall was my dad's, and the master with the two single beds pushed together belonged to my grandparents. One side of the dark, narrow hallway that led to my grandparents' bedroom was decked with a row of family portraits—the other side was brick. I ran my finger on the mortar the way I used to when I was younger. My grandma said I liked to live in the in-between.

The light in their bedroom seeped through gossamer curtains. The sliding glass door offered a side view to the backyard, and I saw the place where she used to grow calla lilies. In that soil, I used to catch pill bugs and bury lizards the cat got to—one time I found a bird skull next to the drainage pipe.

The bookshelf near my grandpa's side of the bed was full of thick bindings, but it was easy to remove the three Bibles he used to study.

"Hokis, Armenia was the first what?" he would ask me.

"Christian nation," I would answer.

A cloud of dust puffed up from the blankets when I placed the heavy books on top of them. I sat on the side of the mattress, then eased onto my back, twisting and resting my spine inside the crack where the two beds met. On the popcorn ceiling above, my head was a small light with loops of plastic crystals. So much of the midcentury home hadn't been altered since they first moved in.

Grandma's silver jewelry box on her nightstand pulled my focus. The springs creaked as I shifted my weight and swung my feet to the other side of the mattress to lift the tarnished, heart-shaped lid. Inside, were a few mismatched pearl earrings, a thin gold chain, and a white gold cross necklace decked with family birthstones. I lifted it out of the box and watched the light catch the different colored stones; the surfaces were cloudy and in need of cleaning. When I found my small piece of aquamarine close to the center, the chain slipped through my fingers and collapsed on the carpet under the bed frame.

In a flash of movement, I slid off the side and onto my knees to reach the necklace, clutching it in my closed, warm palm and pulling it into my chest. My eyes started to burn, and my throat felt thick, mostly from the dust.

I panned my vision under the bed. The fabric from the box spring had dilapidated over the years and stretched into the floor. The space, aside from the stalactites of string, was mostly kept clear. All I found was a red paperboard box by the wall. I reached for it, trying not to send its dense layer of dust flying as I pulled it into the open.

I set the cross necklace onto the bed and let my hands hover over the lid. It was sizable, like the shoeboxes that boots come in, and where my fingers had cleared the gray, a vibrant red peaked through. I hesitated, watching a young, pale silverfish dash off the top. I'd been on three excavations before, one in an ancient burial cave in Madrid. When I was six, my grandma drove through a cemetery to get me to fall asleep for a nap. She slowed the car to a stop as my eyes were closing and pointed out the window. "That's where Papik and I will go, vayri aghjik." It was the first time she called me "wild girl."

Years of training—the patience, ginger handling, dirt removing with brushes and dental picks—escaped me as I folded back the lid. There was a note taped to the inside, and in a nest of shredded kraft paper, rested a blue velvet ring box, a scattering of seashells, dried petals, and assorted rocks. Four small mason jars, the kind she used when my grandma made jam, were burrowed in the paper. Their gold-toned lids were labeled: one for my grandma, one for my grandpa, one for my aunt, and one for my father.

I opened the small, tri-folded note:

Vayri Aghjik,

I trust you with the old ways.

Utem kez, Tatik

My brow furrowed. The closest we'd ever gotten to "the old ways" was rolling dolma and playing backgammon. I let out a huff of air and picked up the navy ring box. Inside, a swirl of gold sat on top of a coiled chain. I held the pendant close to my face: it was the eternity symbol for Hetanism, the Armenian faith before Christianity. I researched it a few years ago when I was getting my master's—the dissertation I wrote ended up getting published, but I never told my family. I peered over my shoulder at my grandparents' wedding portrait. Her dark eyes were shining behind her cheeky smile.

I studied the pendant; the edges were worn and rough in some spots, and one side was more tarnished than the other. A gray hair was caught in the clasp of the chain. A sense of warmth rushed out of my shoulders as I eased the necklace onto my lap.

I lifted the jar with my father's name on the lid out of its paper nest. A cascade of shells and pebbles beat against the bottom of the box, but I was too struck by the contents of the jar to notice. Through the glass, I counted all of his baby teeth, a dark curl of hair secured with a ribbon, and something I guessed could be a dried umbilical cord. I looked at her cheeky grin, then back to the jars. Each had teeth and hair, and she added nail clippings to the ones marked for her and my grandfather. I placed them back into the paper, searching for more instructions or reasons in the process. Without luck, I stared into the eight swirling arms of the pendant.

The half-eaten lizard in the old calla lily bed and the feeling of damp dirt under my fingernails crossed my mind. Grandma watched while she hung up the laundry to air dry, and turned on the hose for my hands, knees, and feet when I was done. "That's good for a lizard," she said and kissed the top of my head as I scrubbed out the soil. "Because it's an animal. People need to be closer to nature."

In Hetanism, the dead are given back to the elements. They're cremated in fire. Then, the ashes are split into three: one portion is buried for the earth, one is thrown into the wind over a gorge or the top of a mountain, and the last is sprinkled into the sea.

Quick footsteps approached the door, and I closed the lid of the box.

"How's it going in here?" Mom asked as she walked into the room. "You ok?"

"Yeah, it's just dust."

"My eyes are bugging me too." She nodded. "You found the red box?"

"Um, yeah, but I'm not ready to open it yet," I told her.

She pointed to my lap. "What's that?"

I lifted the gold necklace. "I found it in her jewelry box with the cross necklace."

"Oh," she smiled. "You should keep it. It's pretty."

"Thanks."

She picked up the stack of Bibles on the other side of the bed, "I'm going to pack these up for Uncle Warren. Did you happen to find any more towels?"

I shook my head. "Sorry, I haven't looked yet."

"It's okay," she said, holding the books to her body. "Bring some out to me when you're done?"

"Yeah, I'll go check the bathroom now." I stood up and placed the box on the bed.

"Don't forget that cross for Allyse." Her eyes caught the glimmer of birthstones. "I was a little sad she didn't give that to you."

The emptiness of the house grew heavy in our silence, and I could see the corners of her mouth start to quake. I waited for sound to escape the barriers of her teeth while I slipped the eternity symbol into my pocket.

"Would you want some coffee?" I asked her. "I can make some once I'm done in here."

"That would be really nice," she answered, flipping the light switch before making her way back through the hallway.

He's Right Behind You – Kevin B (they/them)

We'd go out around one.

Climbing through bedroom windows, we'd try to land softly on bushes and backyard lawns. Some of us went barefoot. Some hid a spare pair of sneakers under porches or tucked under tarps used for covering patio furniture. Some of us just liked being barefoot. It made us feel as though we'd have the strength that comes from mimicking the uncivilized. Some of us would play the whole game with no shoes. No shoes, no shirts. One of us liked to play the game in only his boxer shorts. He would dare anyone to mention his near nakedness. "I'm not gay for running around the woods in my underwear. You're all gay for looking at me in my underwear."

This is teenage logic. Everything is a chess match where both players have only recently discovered how to play Monopoly. Board games were daytime affairs. We would play them by the above-ground pools and in basements while our parents were at work. We were old enough to be home alone, provided we memorized the phone numbers of all the retired neighbors, who could theoretically get to us quickly in the event of an emergency.

Practically speaking, seventy-year-old Mrs. Hasher would not have been able to help any of us had a deranged murderer targeted us the way they did in the cable movies we weren't supposed to watch, but our parents told themselves stories the same way we did. Stories about safety. Stories about good neighborhoods. Stories about how much a locked door could accomplish. Years ago, a girl had been abducted from her home on our street, but the rumor was she opened the door when a stranger knocked. Our parents didn't say it, but they secretly believed that meant she deserved to be kidnapped. "I mean, if your kid is dumb enough to open up the door for just anybody..." They told themselves that we, their children, were smarter than that. Smarter than that girl.

We were not smarter.

We were, in fact, *a lot dumber* than her.

Of course, we didn't know that. We thought we were geniuses. Genius-warrior-punks with wisdom and ferocity, all before our fifteenth birthdays. We believed people were jealous of us, but we didn't know who these people might be. We believed that everyone at school had gone to at least second base, and we were ashamed to have never seen a naked girl in real life. We laughed at the word "condom," but we believed, given the opportunity, that we would be intrinsically fantastic at lovemaking. At school, we had posters in our lockers of Sarah Michelle Gellar and Jennifer Love Hewitt and those of us who had gone to first base had that one poster of Cameron Diaz that would have gotten us suspended if a teacher saw it.

We'd gather at each other's lockers and discuss the arrangements for the game that night. We'd agree on a spot in the woods. Some of us liked meeting at the tree that had been split in half by lighting. Some liked the rock formation that resembled an old man kneeling with his head down. Once the location was agreed upon, we'd argue about the time. Some of us wanted to meet at midnight on the dot. We didn't realize that we were in love with the poetry of it because we swore we hated poetry based on what our teachers had us read. Some wanted to do it later. Much later. Some wanted to meet at three or four so that the game would last until dawn.

"Tomorrow's Saturday. We don't have school. What's the problem?"

The problem was that some of our parents got up around dawn. Some of our mothers would have a heart attack if they woke up and found our beds empty. Some of us didn't want to worry our parents. Some of our fathers used belts if we misbehaved. Some of us cared about our parents too much to let them know what their children were up to at night. Some of us feared our parents more than we feared anything in the woods. Some of us feared nothing. Some of us loved the idea of being gone when our parents woke up. Making them think that we'd escaped. That we were on a runaway train somewhere moving further and further away from them. Some of us liked the feeling of the belt on our skin because it solidified the hate we felt for the people we were meant to love the hardest.

We'd usually meet a little after one. If it was warm out, we'd meet by the lake where the summer camp was before it went out of business. The cabins were still there and the picnic tables and the signs that said, "Mess Hall" and "Nurse's Office." The paint was fading. Vines were growing over the cabin windows. We didn't explore the camp at night. Even the bravest among us weren't that fearless. We'd seen at least one horror movie that took place at a camp, and we didn't want to be chased by a man with a mask.

We only wanted to play a game. In our game, if you followed the rules, you didn't get hurt. Nothing bad happened. If you broke the rules, the game was over for you, but that was it. No injuries. No harm. It was all about stamina. Sustaining yourself throughout the night. There wasn't really any loss. There wasn't even a real way to win. Bragging rights were all we had to play for, and yet, they seemed more valuable than the hundred dollar bills our fathers would leave out on the kitchen counter as though tempting us to steal. Some of us did steal. Some of us felt the belt. Some of us liked it, but we'd never say who.

We started by the lake, and we faced off against each other. Eye-to-eye with another boy standing a foot away from you. That was how it began. We would face each other, take a deep breath, and say—

"He's right behind you."

One of us would say it. The other would listen. Then, the other person would say it—

"He's right behind you."

—And we would escalate the intensity. The rule was that you could not say anything other than those four words, but you could say them however you liked. We could shout them at each other. We could whisper them. Those of us who were more strategic knew that volume wasn't enough. It was about having an action. An objective. It was important to keep a verb in mind.

Beg.

Cajole.

Beseech.

Caution.

Plead.

Convince.

Convince.

Convince.

"He's right behind you."

It didn't matter that we played this game several times a week for two years. It didn't matter that we knew—*we knew*—that nobody was behind us. Inevitably, someone would get spooked. One of us would run home. That first hint of terror was contagious. Soon, more of us would retreat back to our homes. It was rare that more than three or four of us would be left by the end of the night. If your partner ran away, you would find someone else who had also lost their partner, and you would face off against them, speaking the four words. If you were the only one without a partner, you stood silently and waited for someone to leave. Like most boys our age, we had no respect for anything we were meant to respect, and the utmost respect for imaginary things and made-up scenarios. School and church and authority and death were all laughable to us, but this game—this game that we had created out of nothing—this was something to be taken seriously.

None of us could remember who started it. Maybe an older boy who had since graduated from childishly sneaking out of his room at night. Maybe we all put it together like a story composed of hormones and dirty sweat. Maybe it didn't matter. All that mattered was keeping it alive for as long as we could. We never spoke of the game outside of planning it between classes at our lockers. We never talked about who was good at it or bad at it. We never talked about who stayed the longest or who left first. We just played. We played and we never planned to stop playing.

One night, one of us was staring at his partner when he saw the other boy's eyes look slightly to the left. This was against the rules. You only looked at your partner. You used the four words to scare them, if you could. You didn't involve physicality. Not even a slight shift in focus. The other boy began to shake his head. This was wrong. This was against the rules. None of us knew what to do if someone broke the rules, because nobody had ever broken the rules. There were no referees, and, even if there were, it wouldn't have mattered now because there were only two boys left on that night. The other boy appeared to almost choke. He coughed out the words.

"He's right behind you."

The other boy looked as though he was going to raise an arm. Raise a hand. Point to something. Instead, he ran off. The other boy wasn't supposed to run off. You were supposed to wait until the other person said the four words. You were supposed to give them a chance to scare you back. One of us stood there that night, all alone, and felt an immense pride extending down his shoulders and off into the ground below his feet. He was the only one left. A laugh barked past his lips. It was a nervous laugh, but he didn't know where the nerves were coming from, and he wondered if he could get home before his father banged on his door to wake him up for school. If not, it would be the belt, but did that mean anything? He was the last one of us still standing there in the woods.

"He's right behind me."

He didn't know why he said it. It wasn't true. There was nobody behind him. Every sound was natural. Every presence an imagined one. Every instinct to flee was his paranoia trying to torment him now that all his fellow competitors were gone. He would stand in the woods for as long as he liked. He would enjoy this moment.

Despite winning nothing, he would tell himself he was a winner. He was no longer one of us. He was someone else.

"He's right behind me."

But the game was over.

There was nobody left to scare.

Neonatal Cyborg – Elena Sirett (they/them)

Forceps did the hand jive in my mother's torso. She had imagined it all so differently. Had imagined her organs lined up neatly on a table, the coiled snake of her intestine, the half full bladder, the bowel...being...bowel-like? She could never remember what bowels did exactly. She had imagined these pieces removed, her uterus lifted, a tiny familiar face and hands pressed against membrane like Han Solo trapped in carbonite. She had imagined the cut, the removal, the cry, the repair, then the doctor's frowning brow as he tried to remember the exact order of placement, tried to remember how to win at internal organ Tetris. She had imagined being amused by this expression as she held a newborn gurgling daughter to her chest. In reality, the surgery was not an ordered series of removals but rather a concerningly blind rummaging. Through the fog of spinal anesthesia, the gloved hands felt like those of a well-meaning but inexperienced lover. Before blacking out completely, shouts of panic pierced the silence.

I was born too small, too soon, but most importantly, I was born not breathing. I was transferred immediately, without time for human touch, from the grip of turquoise latex to the bed of an incubator.

Incubators are strange contraptions, second mechanical wombs. Closed incubators like mine are mini climates designed to keep fragile newborns alive. See through coffin shaped boxes, sleeping beauty sarcophagi replete with tubes and wires to such an extent you can't help but recall sci-fi, oozing circuitry, the labs of mad scientists. To be an incubator baby is to know from the very start that your existence is technologically assisted, to know from the very start that left to nature's devices, you would not be alive. A cyborg is defined as a hybrid of machine and organism. Cyborg. That is what I am.

"Closed" does not in this case mean "without openings." My incubator has ports at its sides, through which IV's administering blood, medicine and nutrients were fed, sharp needles piercing my centimeter-wide arms. The ports are big enough for adult hands to reach in and help administer the necessary treatments. My father and my mother, once she was sewn back up and standing, could touch me very gently. Holding was of course out of the question. In a few days, I was saved. A nurse who was in the treatment room for the surgery even told her church about me and led a celebratory prayer thanking Jesus for my survival. My parents, an atheist and a lapsed Jew, politely thanked her when she told them. I wonder if that church would still think me a miracle if they saw me now. Like my first birth, my second proved difficult.

Once the doctors deemed me ready for the outside world, prepared for that uncontrolled environment, they gathered. My parents watched from chairs against the walls of the neonatal intensive care unit. For the doctors in the NICU, this was a regular procedure; they expected to lift the lid, remove the tubes and needles, and initiate me into the hold of humanity. However, whilst the "closed" of "closed incubator" does not mean "without openings," it did in my case mean without opening. The doctors at first put on an air of calm, performing so as to not distress the family.

"It's just stuck. This happens all the time!" One said as another scrabbled at the clear sides attempting to find purchase.

This definitely did not happen all the time. The once lidded incubator was now somehow lidless; no matter how many doctors, nurses, administrators and janitors looked, nobody could see where the thing should open. Over the weeks that followed, everything was tried in order to release me safely, but no tool or hand could even leave a scratch on my home. The open sidings where there, but when attempts were made to wrestle my tiny body out through the gaps, the machine's wires came to life; they pulled me in as the humans tried to pull me out, they were so strong, so determined in their grip, that the doctors always stopped for fear of hurting me. In a short time, I grew too large for these rescue attempts.

It's bad being treated like a freak but it's worse being treated like a victim. Do not feel sorry for me. I had a good childhood, a better one than so many. My father taught me to speak and read through the clear plastic. I grew in the safe hold of a controlled space, I never lacked nutrition, I never got sick. It was only years later that I realized the limits of my housing. The incubator's edges pushed up against my burgeoning teenage body, lacerating my thighs, crushing my neck as I curled fetal, trying to fit within its limits. A thigh grew out through one side and an arm through the other, creating a two-limbed, four-wheeled, robot-tentacled creature. The tubing became not caressing, but circulation-cutting, and yet I still do not think myself trapped. Why would I want to go outside, when I know intimately the horrors you people go through? You can hear a lot through the walls of a hospital if you're kept in one long enough. Believe me, I've heard it all. All your gasps, all your tears, all your breaks, fractures, tumors, ruptures, all your unexpected world-inflicted pain. At least in here, in my closed world, the pain is predictable.

My parents stopped visiting. I do not blame them, they lasted almost two decades, it was difficult to see me, they had to move on. They did. They had other normal children and there was just no room for me, the neonatal cyborg. I am mostly left alone now, though there is a nurse whose job it is to make sure that my nutrient tubes stay pumping. They never ask how I feel about that, not that I could answer, acrylic is not membrane, this space is fixed, my face is pressed to numbness against the incubator's walls. My mouth is long past moving.

Synaptic – Christian Barragan (he/him)

It was just past ten o'clock and Hubert could still feel the nanobots undulating beneath his face. He visualized their movements as they danced around the cells of his nervous system. The sleep mask he wore shifted with their clumsy movements before finally falling off.

The little bugs were meant to help him relax and fall asleep, but their incessant writhing was impossible to ignore. No pain, at least. That was clear from the first time they entered his body.

Hubert considered skimming the manual for reassurance, but even his gnawing neuroticism had its limits. He looked at the nightstand where he kept his phone, the nanobots' remote, and his heart medication. Medication he'd hardly taken in weeks. That's what his intruders were there for.

There used to be a point where they worked faster. Now, there he was, spread out on the bed with nothing to do but wait for the insects to work their magic. His breaths steadied until...

His finger twitched.

Stay in your lane! He ran his tongue over the grooves of his teeth and felt...nothing. He frowned. At least, he tried to. He pictured the movements but felt nothing on his face. Back and forth he commanded the muscles in his mouth, but the sensation was minimal. He figured he should...

Knock! Knock! Knock!

The door opened before he could think of anything to say. It was Gladys, his wife, a face that was once enough to calm him. She peeped at him. He wondered if there was any way to exhibit his frustration without speaking. Now he had to start over.

"Oh, you're going to sleep? I'll be out for a while. A friend invited me..."

Hubert stuck an impatient thumb in the air, prompting Gladys to leave. He considered reaching for the meds. Everyone's overstepping tonight. All progress gone. Thump thump thump. Gradually, the voices in his head calmed and his mind filled with emptiness.

Ah.

They still work. His heartbeat finally steadied. He hadn't noticed how strong it was beating. He wondered how he made it this long with such a decrepit organ, but he knew the answer.

...ZZZZZZZZZZZZZZ....

Hubert stirred from what was perhaps the deepest sleep of his life. He awoke sweaty and nervous, his mind racing. Horrible images danced in his head of what he'd just dreamt about. A giant hand inside him, fumbling around his ribcage until grasping the fragile tissue of his heart. POP! His legs flooded with the familiar electric buzz of numbness. Like a column of ants parading on his vulnerable figure.

Hubert put a hand to his bony sternum. Thump thump. Still ticking. He looked to the side of his bed. Gladys wasn't home yet. He would have heard her by now. He nestled back down and grabbed the remote, adjusting the nanobots' settings. Shadows danced in the corners of his room. Time to get some water. After all, he'd already sweat a bucket's worth.

Hubert darted to the kitchen downstairs. He hardly felt anything as the cold liquid sank down into the recesses of his body. He whipped around just as his glass hit the floor and shattered. He could have sworn he saw a dark figure lurking behind the refrigerator. Upon closer inspection, it was clear nothing was there. He checked the lock on the front door just to make sure. Everything in working order, he made haste to clean up the mess.

He heard a car pulling up to the house. Must be Gladys. Now he really needed to go back to sleep. Sounds echoed from outside. His ears quivered with the soft stimuli.

Knock. Creak. Splat.

Meddling kids.

He wanted to go over to the window and yell at them, but it wouldn't do any good. They never listen. He couldn't quite tell what the sounds were anyway. A ball. Someone running. On pavement? No, wood. Like in a house. At this hour? He looked out the window. No one.

Even Gladys didn't take this long to come inside. She was usually content to come straight to bed upon arrival, a fact he dreaded. Hubert hurried back to his room, glancing behind him to make sure the figure hadn't returned. He slipped back into bed, heart pounding.

His face twitched, startling him. He involuntarily whipped his neck around. Now that hurt. The nanobots ought to fix it. A pain rose from his spine into his skull.

Hubert felt an overwhelming frustration for this weak body of his. For his wife who interrupted him. For the kids who wouldn't shut up outside. For the nanobots who weren't doing their job or perhaps working to make things worse.

No, not them. The nanobots had nothing to do with any of that. They were doing everything they could to make him feel better. Just like they were programmed to do.

Hubert froze. Was that really it? Maybe he was just tired. He needed sleep more than anything. He grabbed the remote again and adjusted the settings.

He laid in bed for some time, trying to clear his mind, but it was more active than ever. He reached over to the phone on his nightstand and...swiped it across the room.

Oops.

Before Hubert could begin to retrieve the item, he had a compelling urge to lie back down. No, a forceful urge. Against his will, his muscles pressed him against the center of the bed. His face cascaded with sweat, but he couldn't so much as open his mouth to scream. He felt a wave pulsing through his muscles, as if testing whether they were still there. They felt exhausted as if they'd been endlessly yanked by the tendons. They still kept him on the bed.

His heart raced like a tired engine dying out, ready to burst in spectacular fashion. He tried with what desperation he could muster to reach for the pill bottle, but his arm wouldn't move. His chest heaved dramatically.

His mind calmed as Gladys finally opened the door. A tranquility befell his muscles as the sense of dread seeped out of him. Every one of them ached, but they obeyed his command. He rested his smarting head deep into his pillow and closed his eyes, trying to make sense of the past events.

"Hon, are you asleep?"

What a stupid question. How could he answer if he was asleep? His throat was sore, any exertion would hurt but she'd only keep asking if he remained quiet. He needed to tell her what happened. He opened his eyes, but his mouth wouldn't budge. She stood there, doughy-eyed, as a familiar panic swarmed through Hubert's being. His exhausted heart pumped a sense of impending doom throughout his body.

"I'm going to be in the living room for a while. Are you okay in here?"

...

"Yes dear, everything's fine."

Gladys's face lit up with joy as she shut the door, inverse to the horror spreading across Hubert's.

Those weren't his words.

The Thief of Bayfalls – Sebastian Vice (he/him)

With Bayfalls sinking into the sea, and death warrants out on my ass, I should be hiding in a cargo ship for the Jeweled Isle of Giles. My employer insists on retrieving *The Grimoire of Gremalor*. I'm not positive what Gremalor is. I'm not paid to ask questions, but tales would have me believe it to be a sword from the Void.

My perch on an abandoned apartment sways too much for my liking. Gotta move.

It's raining harder than normal. The streets are flooded, men and women rowing past in boats. The city is in full pandemonium.

I hop to the next building and as I get my footing my previous perch collapses, a blade caressing my throat.

"You little shit." I recognize that voice.

"Willa," I say. Don't let the name fool you. Ice flows through her veins. Cuddle up with her and you'll bleed to death. "A pleasure as always."

"Last I heard you were the most wanted man in these parts," she smirks, removing the blade at my neck.

"Last I heard, you died."

"Can't kill me that easy, darling," she winks. "You're after *The Grimoire*?"

Damn the gods. If she knows, who else? My good for nothing employer said it was a secret. So much for trust, or reliability.

I shake rain from my coat. "Who can say?"

"It's in the temple. I got a contract to assassinate a priest."

It would be odd for her to open up like this, but we have a habit of stumbling into one another. She doesn't get in my way, I don't get in hers. We don't particularly fancy each other, but sometimes interests converge. We've saved each other's asses more than a few times.

Willa licks the blade. "Say we work together? Mutual benefit and all?"

I shrug. "Sure. Rumor has it we got less than an hour before this gods' forsaken city goes under."

She slaps me on the back. "Move your ass, Toad."

I hate that name.

***

The temple's half underwater. Lucky for me, the library's on the third level. I'd have preferred to scope the place out. This kind of heist takes weeks to devise a plan. Given the rain as of late, I had three days.

The glass roof is broken and screams echo in the distance. Willa smiles amidst the chaos. Women like her thrive on disorder. I suppose it makes assassination easier.

My worry is the condition of the Grimoire. Rain's pouring through like a waterfall. The library better be intact. This book's my ticket to retirement.

Willa smacks her lips. "Have fun, darling. I know I will." We peer down at guards ushering people out. "I'll clean up any riff raff. Thank me later with a cut from the book."

She jumps down before I can say anything. Bodies splash into water. I've yet to meet a more efficient killer. I fall down with all the grace of a rag doll. I'm getting too old for this shit. Not so nimble anymore. Don't know how Willa does it.

"Lying in filth like a pig," she says, extending her hand, yanking me from a pool of water. "Losing your edge, Toad."

I massage my shoulder. "Good thing I'm retiring."

She lets out a chuckle, "Said that last time we met, around three years ago." Willa bolts while I'm looking for the library. The rate of water rising gives me less than an hour.

I stumble into a room with shelves of books and close the door. I guess *this* is the library. Dry for now. No windows. Candles burn on a desk, and I grab one to illuminate the shelves.

It's a thick book with a red sword on the spine. I think, or so my employer had told me. He thinks, does he? He could barely get the words out between mugs of beer.

After longer than I'd like, I find the book. I hope. The sword is on the spine, and faded. And it's not red, but blue. I rotate it looking for words that aren't there. This better be the book.

I tuck it in my pack, to go looking for Willa. Second floor is completely flooded. It'll be minutes until the third follows suit.

Willa smacks my head. "Let's go, Toad."

***

I'm hiding out in an attic somewhere. Willa had a boat ready, but got herself riddled with arrows on our departure. I won't shed tears, sure she once killed a king, but she's also knifed an old woman retired from farming.

Somehow I escaped without the book getting too damaged. I'll have to move soon, but conditions need to get worse so guards stop looking.

I managed to pick up a few languages in Bayfalls over the years, but I don't recognize what's written here. I thumb through drawings of an ebony woman riding a black dragon. The sword looks nice. If I had to guess, you'd need two hands to wield it.

I really wanted to see what the inside of the void looked like. The wizards keep a tight lip, and speak dialects only they understand. Alas, I'm left wanting. My employer thinks only one person has ever seen the inside of the void, but he peddles rumors like he peddles watery piss as beer. Anyway, apparently Karlaka, Last Daughter of Void Star, was the only such person.

I can sense the water rising. Time to slither aboard my employer's ship *The Crimson*. Fence the book, get paid, retire in the Jeweled Isle, and meet a lovely man to marry.

***

I board *The Crimson* as the city sinks beneath the surface.

"Who are you?" A deckhand asks.

"Unfortunately they call me Toad."

"I don't know you."

The stench of bravado tempts me to stab this bastard in the eye. My employer wouldn't like that though. Willa doesn't have as much restraint as me. If only she were here.

"Tell the Captain I'm here."

"Toad?"

I nod.

Fights break out in the smaller boats. Several people are stabbed and thrown over. The sea is like a garden of ships and other vessels. I hope they aren't headed to Giles. I need my reputation sullied like I need my pockets picked.

A few rafts approach *The Crimson* and attempting to board. Poor bastards end up turning the sea pink. I didn't stab anyone. Violence is a tool of the impulsive.

The deckhand returns post-fight, "Captain'll see you."

***

I slump down in a velvet chair in the Captain's quarters. He's sipping wine, pouring over papers. Nice office. King size bed. Bookshelf. And a parrot flying around. A wealthy merchant told me this guy's banned from setting foot on any land. Another time I'd ask if he yearns to feel soil between his toes.

I remove the book from my sack and set it on the desk. "The Grimoire of Gremalor."

He squints through his glasses. "It's stained."

Now the agreed upon price of fifty thousand coins becomes twenty five thousand. My price is final. Think I give a shit about the condition?

He throws a satchel at me. I thumb through the coins. Ten thousand.

"You're short."

The man leans back. "And the book is damaged."

Before I can protest, an echo of bodies hitting the deck causes the captain to flee. I pocket the coins and the book.

Silence.

A hand grips my shoulder.

"You have my book." I turn to an ebony woman with dreadlocks pulled back in a ponytail. Just like in the picture, a sword—perhaps Gremalor—hums at her back.

I bolt to the side of the room, hugging the wall. "Karlaka?"

She nods, "I prefer diplomacy to raw strength."

I gesture to the door. "The men out there dead?"

"My preferences aren't always met."

"I need to get paid."

She closes her hand around my throat, lifting me into the air. I may or may not soil myself.

"It's—yours." I choke.

She releases me, and I slam to the ground. Fumbling through my pack, I fling the book at her.

Her voice is cold, indifferent. "Name?"

"Toad."

"Toad," she says, cradling the book. "You know too much."

"I don't. I don't know the language." I pause. "And if asked, I don't know you. In fact—"

Her eyes tighten, burning with ice. "—you know too much. You have a choice. Die here, or come with me into the Void."

Not much of a choice, eh? I've always wanted to see the void. I'm told all magic flows from it.

"The Void."

She waves her hand, opening a portal that pulsates purple. "Follow me."

NON FICTION

Cigarette Clouds – Annie Williams (she/her)

- I -

Cigarette clouds rise to the ceiling fan as my mom, my neighbor, Sandra, and I play 500 rummy. My mother brings the brown tip to her thin lips, taking a slow drag from her cigarette. She lays down a run, gaining 15 points. She sets her cards down for a second, not realizing she's exposing her hand. "Ah shit," she laughs, then quickly flips them over and laughs a little more while sipping vodka. It doesn't matter though cause I draw a card, lay down three aces, and withdraw, emptying my hands and scoring big.

"Damn," Sandra says as she starts to search her pockets for her pack of Montegos.

My mother blinks in surprise. "What the hell?" She lights up another Marlboro. I laugh, take in my glory and watch as they count their negative points

- II -

My brother pulled out a cigarette and lit it up with shaky hands, all while watching the fire with his red doe eyes. He yells, "Get an ashtray." I didn't have time to think and didn't know where mom put hers, so I handed him a small plate from the kitchen, decorated with blue flowers. We locked eyes, and he chuckled, "You've been hanging with hood niggas haven't you." But still, he takes it, sprinkling ashes over the flower. I wanted to tell him no, that I'm not like him, pretending I'm from the streets as if our parents hadn't given us this house alongside their blood, but I didn't. I sat on the chair, staring at him as smoke left his mustached, chapped lips, wondering if I should wake up my parents or let them have peace for once.

- III -

At the Christmas party at Grandma's, I run downstairs to meet a gust of gray smoke coming from the basement. My aunts and uncles drink their whiskey and Bud Light between puffs. Even though I'm allowed down here, I feel as if I'm in the VIP section of a club without my pass. I glide through the smoke and people, reaching over to my dad who is the only sober adult at the party. "When we will go home?"

He tells me we will still be awhile, meaning we'll stay until almost one in the morning. So, I leave the nicotine-flavored fog and head upstairs where I can feel fresh air on my neck from the open windows. My cousins are in one room playing Cards Against Humanity. Laughing at crude sex jokes and adult things I don't quite understand. But I don't really care, and just want to focus on evolving Combusken into Blaziken. I find the designated coat room, the blue room with coats piled on the bed. I sit on the floor and battle Watson, the electric gym leader. After using double kick, Watson's final Pokemon HP falls to zero. I grin and I kick my feet and throw my hands in the air. In the midst of my celebration, I take a glance at the picture on the wall. It's two white ladies in their flapper dresses, dangling cigarette holders in their petite hands.

- IV -

Magenta and her friends sit in her dark plum room, smoking their USBs that have a hint of bubblegum and watermelon to them. Still, I smell the nicotine from their futuristic cigarettes making my nose itch, but I'd rather have this than watching them pop powder pink pills and pass a joint around. Weed smells even worse, and the pills make them go into a dance with death on the floor, twisting their bodies like inexperienced b-boys, with Lil Peep playing in the background.

- V -

My parents and I, along with my mom's coworker, were in the parking lot of Joanne's on a random fall night when I first got my cat, Ziggy. He was a small, fragile thing wrapped up in a blanket, mom's coworker cradling him like a baby. She explained to me that Ziggy was rescued from a smoker's home, making me wonder if it's a coincidence or not that his fur is the color of ashes falling from a factory chimney's cloud. Mom and Dad stared at the tiny feline, Mom's eyes sparkling in excitement, Dad seemingly occupied with calculating how much a pet would cost. My mom gathered him into her arms, and I leaned over a little, wanting to pet him but too busy staring in disbelief at how adorable he was. He still had the scent of nicotine in his fluffy fur, and his green eyes were buggy. Probably thinking who the hell these people were.

- VI -

My grandma sits next to me in the backyard of her cabin. Papa is in the forest gathering wood while their pit bull, Lucious, lays on the grass, letting the sun soak into his thin, brown fur. She smokes one of her Parliaments as I tell her my 20-year-old worries: paying for college, deciding whether to live on campus or not, finding a new job, figuring out who my real friends are, and how I've cutted a few times on my thighs. The scent of nicotine stings my nose, while the cherry pop stings my lips, but the thing that stings like a big ol' wasp is when my grandma asked, "Why do you cut yourself?" I have no idea, Grandma. Still trying to solve that riddle with my therapist.

- VII -

After dad left for his midnight shift, as we sat in the living room, I almost told my mom how much I've been wanting to die. How all the pills in our cabinets looked so tasty. Instead, I distracted myself with an unexpected truth, "I've been wanting to try a cigarette." Maybe because I was so distraught or maybe because she was glad to hear I'd never smoked, she pulled out her Marlboro's and handed me one. I looked at her fingers, then her eyes. "Really?" I asked.

My mom shrugged, "Better than smoking something else." With my sweaty palms, I took the cigarette out of her hands and put it between my dry, chapped lips. She sat down next to me, passed me a purple lighter, and watched me take my first and last smoke. I took it in gently and let it out, surprised I didn't choke. Then again, being a visual learner around smokers all my life, of course, I got it right. What surprised me most though was that it wasn't bad, but it also wasn't good. It tasted like the color beige. "What do you think?" Mom asked me as I tried another puff.

"I don't know…I was just expecting something…more I guess?"

My mom laughed as she took the lighter. "Yeah, nothing really special, huh?" A cigarette cloud escapes her lips, "It doesn't help much either."

Practicing Nature - Lara Konrad (she/her)

Yes, inside the small, cozy attic hotel room in Vienna, late afternoon, almost evening, just after we had returned from walking around the city for some time, have shared a bowl of pancake soup and an order of goulash while seated next to each other in one of the deep, well-upholstered cafe booths, have had sex, and now, lying arm in arm in bed, we're talking—fantasizing—once again, about the future.

Once back in Mexico City, how we'd get rid of my roommate Marie, eventually, as soon as possible—recently engaged, soon she'd hopefully move all of her things to Dallas, Texas for good—and then turn the already perfectly laid-out Mario Pani apartment into our perfect love nest: our home.

Money in our dreams of a joint future didn't exist, wasn't mentioned, so we'd get that wooden pair of Josef Hoffmann armchairs we saw at the antique shop earlier that day—place them in the cavity adjacent to the dining area.

And maybe get the metallic lamp, *yes? Yes, Yes.*

And the dark-green armoire, and the stone side table we spotted at the Dorotheum. And the pair of tall candle holders, which would certainly calm the impressive, disquieting skyline that unfolds inside the living room's floor-to-ceiling window, and have children.

Two? Three?

Definitely more than one.

For every child should have a sibling, so it feels a little less alone in the world—an enduring opinion I can't remember having said aloud that afternoon in bed. Neither, in fact, do I recall one of us specifying the exact number of humans we'd produce.

Reciprocally, the word, the destination, was somehow just expelled into the room, into the open, into life, *children*, as if it were the most obvious subsequent step to complete or cement our month-old romantic-domestic bliss.

The only other additional step, besides—after—acquiring a house in the countryside: blue walls, our individual studios separated by a courtyard filled with trees, trees that'd periodically cover the ground with leaves, and fallen fruit. Fallen, rotten fruit. Figs, mostly. Rotten, trampled figs whose flesh's sweet, earthy odor would travel throughout the air most poignantly in the early morning—alongside the crowing of roosters, bestowing the incoming day with exceptional possibility.

Then and there—yes, inside the hotel room, inside the softened starched bedsheets while encircled by warm orange light, light that emanated from each corner, left and right, that so very sheltering and somehow melancholy light that emanated from each corner's nightstand, yes, then and there—this was the very first time I verbalized the idea of having children.

What did this agreement actually feel like?

The sudden absent presentiment of getting an abortion: before Carlos, before having entered my thirties, before (especially female) life is supposed to change, is supposed to transfigure, a planned, silent solution harbored confidently by my insides—as much as it's possible to imagine, to conclude, the unknown—ever since I started having sex at nineteen—should there rise the absurd occasion of turning out fertile while on the pill.

An abortion, yes, no doubt, despite whatever painful consequences.

Until the time has come, is right, I would reason, trying to soothe myself whenever an abrupt anxiety of being pregnant erupted days before finally spotting the awaited stain of blood in my underwear, feel it drop.

With Matthew and Sander, Daniel, and Elliott: an abortion, for sure, until I'd no longer be a college student.

With Sigurd: until we'd have money, and know what it is that we actually want to do with our lives, outside of being in love.

An abortion, yes, for sure, *until it is time.*

***

Death. In fact, just like death: I think, I continue to realize.

Until the playground incident, until Gisela (my so-called therapist), until almost exactly three full summers ago (at that point: no longer in a relationship, not with Carlos, not with anyone) when a presumably light, presumably trivial observation of mine while walking in the park shifted, shifted into something else, has begun to quietly pulsate ever since as a revelation, a reality, autonomously like death did the assumption of having children one day reign the future of my being: natural, inevitable, beyond grasp, and, thus—so it seemed, until recently, until now—beyond the inner demand for (re)consideration.

Like death, a certitude that simply seemed to coincide with the act of having been born. Born female.

Born homeless—by which I mean lonely.

***

Not once, actually, not ever in my life have I envisioned their faces. Their sweet tender voices—calling, laughing.

Not once, no, have I imagined myself embracing them, swaying my fictitious children in the crook of my arm from side to side; playing with their fine, possibly blonde hair.

Never have I imagined the color of their skin. Their eyes.

Blowing air on their skinned tiny knees.

After the hotel room in Vienna, after I was in love once again, after I was sure to have finally found the man of my dreams, the man of my realest and most feasible of dreams: Carlos: my awaited destiny after years and years (six, to be precise) of being unable to attach to any man after my first and only great love had ended at twenty-five, occasionally—twice, at least, that's what I can remember for now—images would arrive of me standing by a kitchen counter and neatly packing their sandwiches into plastic zip bags; waiting for them outside school.

Waiting outside the school gate, I saw myself as a woman, a stranger, a woman whose time to live her interiority had organically run its course, met its expiration date. A matured woman, in a long, cream-colored trench coat, car keys in hand, patiently waiting, a warm distant smile framing her matured, stalled face, not satisfied, no, not fulfilled, but consoled: relieved—waiting like time no longer existed, like time no longer mattered.

Waiting like the future had been conquered.

What did I think was going to happen to my writing: I don't know. In my former vision of domestic dailiness I didn't think this far ahead.

I might have even secretly entertained the vague notion of no longer writing—no longer needing to write, write in order to exist.

If I'd write once married with children, I'd simply write to pass the time. Quaint, useless little poems about the garden, and the flowers. Write in order to overcome the soft, sweet quiet boredom in the afternoon, or in the late morning, once the children had been dropped off at school, and I had planned out lunch.

***

One by one, yes, and slowly, quite slowly, slowly yet gradually but especially as of late, these past couple of months, just as I'm approaching my thirty-sixth year on this earth, these feelings and thoughts that have started to progressively emerge, rise up, ever since three summer ago Gisela remarked in her office that, *Ah(hh)*— her mouth momentarily slightly ajar, a timeless gap, an indefinable space between life and time, a kind of space that somehow always surrounds us when she's about to reveal something—motherhood wouldn't suit me, *actually*, wouldn't suit my nature, my personal nature that apparently desires, if not commands**,** freedom—

independence—after I briefly and only mentioned that moment in the park, that mere instant of taking in that woman at the playground.

After I merely mentioned the thought that had abruptly crossed my mind the moment my eyes had spontaneously lifted from the book's page as I walked by the enclosure and my gaze had landed on a young kneeling mother who absentmindedly ran sand through her fingers in order to keep the dazed toddler next to her entertained.

How at that moment of taking in her lethargic gaze and her lethargic hands and her wilted torso, I had silently said to myself with a mutual calm presence of anxiety as well as relief that *I'd hate to be her*—not HER, but her her: for my thoughts, my mind, no longer to be my own.

Especially now, I then had figured, that Carlos (any boyfriend, any romantic interest) had stopped dominating most hours of my days.

Now that the unnecessary drama, the terror, was moving more and more away from me, into the past, making space for the present: the gentle patches of sun in the cool morning shade, the weightlessness of my feet and legs and arms, the walk, the trees, the sporadic smell of jasmine, the novel reflections of one of my favorite contemporary authors that swooningly thrusted me that particular morning even further inside the world.

***

Set aside the by-now discovered fact how startlingly little, how so very, very little, essentially never, I preoccupied myself with the subject of creating children, this subject that no more or less was bound to outline the rest of my life, what's been especially remarkable, dear reader, what's been most peculiar, bewildering in fact, is that throughout this slow, slow three-year-old contemplative pilgrimage away from motherhood—a sometimes more, sometimes less daunting, yet evidently more and more necessary, that is to say sincere, personal task—my intimate truth didn't, and still hasn't, hit me in the face, not this time.

Not as one might expect.

Not like it has happened in the past. With New York, or Carlos—other instances when presumably secured futures were all of a sudden extracted from myself, when just as involuntarily I suddenly acknowledged their overall inadequacy in relation to my innate way of being.

No, this time the truth, my truth, hasn't dismantled me to bits and pieces—not fundamentally.

Not at all was there that instantaneously physical feeling of sinking. Was there a force (not right then: at my therapist's office, not later, not now: here at my desk) to protest, claim the contrary, somehow convince the outside as much as myself that what had been uttered, what had been claimed, wasn't actually true.

No, not like it happened with Carlos—when, almost automatically, I began to list some of the many things we had in common. *But the music, the taste in furniture.* No.

This time I just sat there, inside the room, at my therapist's office, took in her comment, a faint pause, must have held my breath, but then just continued conversing, continued speaking as if nothing, absolutely nothing, had changed.

There was this dread, though. There was this dread, you see.

That dread that somehow continues to haunt and mesmerize me. This momentary, tranquil nonetheless intense dread that flooded my body. Several hours after my session with Gisela had ended, in the evening, during my habitual stroll through the English Garden.

Yes, that dread. For of course there's something at stake, dear reader, always and always, the moment we acknowledge a truth outside expectation—whatever its kind: whether the expectation is a product of nature or nurture, whether the expectation is loud, still loud, or has quieted down, has been tamed.

The habit, the faith: yes, the faith is somehow always there.

**

That dread.

By then, I realize, I realize now as I am trying to write this essay, trying to think through this certainly peculiar and this particularly complex and ongoing experience of facing up to one's own authentic humanity, already I was too much on the path of becoming who I am.

So no longer was it actually the customary pain of loneliness that coursed through my body later on that evening during my walk through the park—the instant Gisela's remark about motherhood began to consciously register all over my system.

The presence of loneliness, yes, the unbearable presence of homelessness, of selflessness, which in the past has been most often a guide for choosing and enduring and returning to (over and over and over again) all kinds of impossible landscapes. Has made me place unwavering trust in the horizon of certain things, living as well as inanimate things, worldly things, certain everyday mythologies, without questioning them—not ever seriously asking myself whether in reality, outside the illusory future, these things ought to receive my dedication.

Yes, indeed, the absence of loneliness that suddenly enables me to regard and feel life clearly, soberly.

By and by.

The total absence of loneliness which has granted the chance to start recognizing that motherhood—and in that case, too, the goal, *the goal*, of getting married—was indeed most probably only ever somehow fastened to the innate desire to arrive, to rest.

To arrive: to arrive, I think, I try to remember, at the permanent moment in time, the situation, where—yes, yes yes—no longer I must venture out into the world and scavenge it for meaning.

For once married with children, so I had assumed, so I expected, so, periodically, during whatever stretches of companionlessness, I would nostalgically behold young families dressed in white on Sundays at the cafe where I'd usually end up working in order to fill or forget time, life would start: would stop, would stop to constantly require me to conjure purpose—life—from within.

Automatically it would exist outside of me.

All I'd need to do is wake up in the morning, open my eyes. Sit down at the breakfast table, have it unfold.

Yes, indeed, the miraculous institution of domesticity that would relieve me from myself.

Now, in hindsight, on further reflection, however ridiculous my former assumption, however I, however pathetic, (still) it makes sense to me why I put all my faith into the opposite of aloneness, put all my faith into the external, for until having gotten here: capable of actually sensing myself exist—the who, not the what—the presumed me, a *me* almost entirely disconnected from the core of its being, was under the plain, eternal and constant impression that *inside* this is as best as it gets—a useless carcass that would experience occasional pangs of artificial joy—what underneath, farther down, always ever really resonated as a form of relief—when deeming herself desirable in the new top or sweater while standing in front of the mirror; when there was a new man she liked, she wanted, somebody to put her quiet, rather undefined hopes in: just somebody else to inspire her to live.

Morning, dawn.

The incorporeal, boundless gift of morning, or the essence of human company, started to arrive, become available, when...? When ever since the pandemic's outbreak I was impelled, ultimately impelled, to stop clinging to the surface, falling and falling and falling (not as long as one might suspect, might fear), when from thereon after having steadily fallen inwards for a while, it eventually got quieter and quieter, got so quiet or calm, right now it feels as if that new silence is most accurately described in the way of me forgetting that I exist: the world, the outside, Instagram, people: emptied images.

Everything is what it solely is.

No longer is there that soft, underlying burn to exchange lives. Despite whatever.

Despite their..., their..., their... At this instant I can't seem to mentally conjure a genuine example of what in the past would have especially given me a reason to daydream, to wish and wait for.

The Danish chef and his model wife and the new dog and the second or third baby—just people, yes, just people now who are being people.

The wealthy, young gallerist. Just wealthy, just young.

***

Considering the tacit longstanding prospect to be having children some day, *yes, yes: one day*, what's also somewhat shocking to discern is how on that warm summer evening at the park—the very first moment I made actual contact with yet another plausible dimension of my destiny—I wasn't saddened by the unexpected possibility of not becoming a mother.

No.

To my total surprise, I was not somehow profoundly lacerated (nor am I now) by the sudden idea of missing out on that unique human-to-human connection—what that kind of love, that instinctual devotion, would feel like.

Actually, coming to think of it: that one evening, that evening of that notable dread, my mind (according to my memory) didn't even go there, attended in any way the thought of missing out on that transformative experience.

That bond.

Certainly that bond must be awesome, wondrous.

Must be comforting, that permanent bond: I have imagined, now and then—more than anything.

With a seemingly heightened sense of nostalgia did I just regard my oldest niece crawl on top of my sister's lap this past Saturday. Both of their long, long hair in a long, long ponytail, lusciously waving back and forth. Their simultaneous proclivity for public attention.

Yes, somehow momentarily desirous of this doubling, this extension—the more and more my niece has started to speak, becomes a person. Becomes a refuge. To be my sister, sitting on the picnic blanket—in any event, in the event of a tragedy: to have that refuge, that apparently ever-growing, ever-evolving refuge, that pretend fortress, I felt myself thinking while handing over the bowl of strawberries. Being able to flee, hide, hide a little better from pain.

Hide for some time, be able to maybe hide forever.

Yes, somehow still this pale impression that people with spouses and children are not immune to sorrow but will be able to traverse it more gently.

Bury their sorrow into loving, loving the people that are closest to them—the people that will continue to exist, those people who will hopefully outlive them. When it is time, though, why wouldn't one be able to find shelter in friendship. I wonder. Solemn friendship. Or nature. Birds and trees, the wind, the barely audible sound of wind on my favorite park bench: ever since the last breakup, ever since not being inside a romantic relationship, not fixated on a specific person, and after having vanquished the loneliness, yes, that great loneliness, these are some of the things I find myself having opened up to appreciating, enjoying, noticing.

Suddenly all this space, that patience, yes, that sudden capacity to hold time while in the company of my parents' neighbor, or the cashier lady at the supermarket.

This strange, still somewhat novel experience of having those unspectacular, minute encounters be enough. Flush me with gratuitous joy.

No—to be completely honest, not even these past many moments, these past many days, as I have been contemplating a new kind of future, considering it this directly, touching my sister's newly growing belly nothing inside announces itself as envy: as grief—the kind of painless longing I may always feel when walking or driving through the deep countryside, traveling past small garden gates of houses, simple wooden houses that lead to opened shutters and their opened windows and opened doors and abandoned garden tables under old trees.

My incapability to long for the more obvious, the supposedly more meaningful: a relatively familiar awareness that now while seated here at the desk—at this very instant of writing, of thinking aloud—as well as anytime my hands embrace my sister's life, makes me grow a little uneasy, ashamed, for it strikes as strangely monstrous, unnatural, yes, somehow unwomanly, to love without simultaneously detecting the intimate urge to own, to hold, to claim: to keep.

No, I have never felt envy.

No, not now, not three years ago, not seven—when my first niece was conceived: not even then, no, when I was still riddled with all that acute loneliness: when all I knew was how to abide.

What I felt the first time was shock. Loss.

An innocuous, painless sensation of loss. Jealousy, I always suppose(d): my older sister, whose affection to this day I probably most yearn and strive for. The first pregnancy test dangling on the computer screen in front of me three or four months after the wedding, on command I obediently conjured excitement for the camera.

The same way, coming to think of it, when they got engaged— as if I could perfectly relate to their enthusiasm, could detect within me, deep within me, beyond the loneliness, beyond the desire to arrive, the indirect, ancient desire to rest, to watch rather than the desire to be witnessed, detect within me that same sincere aspiration.

***

Reader, the dread of freedom.

At the park, that evening at the park, meanwhile I couldn't resist projecting my newly-acknowledged, inescapable nature into the near and distant future, the sudden dread.

If really born to be childless, and thus husbandless (at least in the traditional sense, bound to the same household, day in, day out, night after night after night): god, the dread.

Yes, that's right.

On that summer evening, evacuated from all familiar forms of loneliness, the instant I admitted out of nowhere that Gisela's comment might be right, might hold true, that yes, in actual fact, I cherish my privacy, I now so dearly and clearly appreciate my interiority, the silence and the time, the vast, disinhibited silence and time to feel and to think, so sharply, so nakedly I could suddenly sense myself dreading human

freedom—the unabashed, naked reality of eternal freedom that for the first time unfolded itself ahead of me inside the park just as I was about to cross the small bridge in order to make it up the steep hill.

By myself: so clearly, so definitely, so quietly I assumed myself sentenced to live. The utterly naked, seemingly daunting task—I now remember dreading, placidly, for it is useless, and certainly less maddening (I had learned by then), to rebel against one's fate—to rise every single morning from this point forward, day after day after day, and have everything, absolutely everything, all of life, so clearly and so nakedly depend on me. Entirely, thoroughly responsible for how I feel: all the light. So utterly responsible for all the light to come in, to come through.

Me: the sole author of my doing, my being, forever and always.

The very same reason, I suspect, I know—secretly, intimately, I must have always known—why I dreaded (and sometimes, often, still do) and avoided my writerly vocation for as long as possible.

Since writing, the same as freedom—personal: audienceless: limitless freedom—demands the best of me. Demands the truth.

Only is attainable, you see, becomes surmountable, lovable, perhaps not always but almost always, becomes a state of grace as soon and as long as it aligns with the inside—the most inner depth of my being—where pure life takes place. An unavoidable collaboration between the internal and external that's mostly laborious during its inception phase—when the noise still is loud, is loudest: when all types of small voices encourage I come back, exist outside of myself, give in to whatever trivial or tremendous ready-made distraction that at the end, and usually to begin with, served no other objective but to disconnect, disconnect from being me: from being.

That lessened, much, much lessened, yet continuous, daily pull—yes, to slip away into passivity: to be led.

Perhaps most especially during a weekday summer afternoon, or early evening—the small hours when the tedious mildness of life can seem almost hardest to endure, to embrace.

The especially great task, yes, to consciously honor time when there are no imminent plans in the days, weeks to come.

No birthday party, no dinner. No concert. No book awaiting in the letterbox.

Nothing to look forward to—nothing apparently grand or exciting to strive for. Yes, yes, dear reader. On that evening unbarricaded of all kinds of (tangible and intangible) illusions, sensitive for the first real time to our inborn constant solitary spirit, so very plainly I recognized then as much as I do now—now, three years later, today—that if I want to live, I myself must live.

That if I want to be here, inside life, I myself must choose to get up every morning and from then onwards must choose at every new heartbeat of the day to reconnect, connect, connect—participate, participate actively whenever I want to be alive outside the fact of having been born.

Make that oddly, initially exhausting yet ridiculously simple choice over and over and over and over and over again to come back, here, inside this body, breathe, breathe in and out, succumb to the trustworthy void.

Instead of running downstairs now, buy half a loaf of bread and honey and cold, cold butter to then stuff my face while once more ending up playing movie after movie after movie, as a true "reward" (rather than a liberation, rather than a paralyzation) for having attended this essay during these past many days and many weeks, I ought to choose to continue embracing my relentless freedom, my wild, sweet, naked, limitless freedom, do what in reality, in real time, I actually like to do, which is to grab the book from the entryway and head over to the park, sit down on my favorite bench.

My recently discovered favorite bench because it is the only one without a trashcan next to it. On its own, directly it faces an unspectacular gathering of big and small wild trees, undergrowth really, through which the pleasant, no longer burning, sun settles.

The light. The light. How to describe the light, dear reader, dear friend, that imbues the body, imbues it each time, just shortly after one has chosen to withhold the seismic, senseless impulses of wanting, of forgetting, of dreading, the pressure, the apparent supposed pressure, all that egoic, identity-driven expectation, has somehow managed to wait it out, rode through whatever measure of discomfort—sooner or later, finds oneself here within the light, yes, that's right, not in front of it, not encircled by it, but actually alongside with it, no longer even a spectator, a watcher, an admirer—just finds oneself enmeshed with the entirety of nature.

The meaningless light, yes, yes. Always that gentle, peaceful, unexpected light.

We All Live in a Pokémon World - Kashawn Taylor (he/him)

One of my earliest memories is of my grandma whipping across Connecticut on a Sunday after church, me buckled in the back seat, anxious, excited, and hopeful. We visited several familiar red K-Marts and fewer, similarly, friendly blue Walmarts on a quest to find a copy of the new *Pokémon Yellow* for Gameboy Color. It was like she and I were researchers chasing an elusive species of animal which had only been spotted in the wild once or twice. The frantic pace of our race across the state was exhilarating like taking a cold shower or touching a hot burner on the stove.

After so many let-downs, we rolled into the parking lot of yet another superstore—Sears, maybe, or Caldor—the afternoon sun beaming through the crank-handle windows of my grandma's old, white Chrysler with the star emblem. She looked back at me and said, "This is the last store."

I searched the sealed cases behind which said, "Gameboy games." Nothing. Disheartened, but not yet depleted of hope, I double-checked, then checked the cases reserved for games of the most current consoles like the original PlayStation. People made mistakes, and maybe the shelve stockers placed the game in the wrong section…Nothing. I craned my neck to scan the enormously high top shelves, thinking the ladder to reach so high must be super tall.

Nothing.

Deflated, I made my way through the aisles like a balloon come untied, searching the ground once more before I found my grandma at the electronics department's checkout counter. In that prophetic way that parents know, she *knew*, and wrapped a matronly arm around me. Tears streaked my cheeks in salty rivulets as I squeezed her back, my short arms encircling as much of her soft, comforting midsection as I could reach.

The cashier asked what we were looking for. She told him. He frowned.

"That's a tough one to find, huh? We might be sold out." He flashed me a tiny, pitiful smile. "But I'll look in back for you, buddy." He disappeared through a swinging door labeled EMPLOYEES ONLY located between wall displays of top-of-the-line VCRs and expensive, new gadgets called DVD players.

An eternity-and-a-half passed before the door swung wide open again, and he emerged with a small square box with Pikachu in all his electrifying yellow-and-black glory on the front, looking ready to battle.

***

When, in January 2023, I heard an inmate shout, "Yo! They added *Pokémon* to the tablet!" I was more than a bit skeptical. Five months deep on a three-year bid, I was thoroughly acquainted with the painfully outdated Securus Android tablets. The damn near indestructible bricks of antiquated technology had clear casing showcasing wiry internal organs; they weighed at least a solid pound. It surprised me more people weren't brained with them on a weekly basis.

Due to exorbitant fees for "content" and "delivery" most offerings cost more than their worth. After fees, a 99-cent song came out to $2.10. Not only did Securus rape us and our families for money, they confounded us with an unfriendly user interface. Our only consolation came in the form of overpriced, cheaply-made knock-off games like *Super Mike*, *Temple Rush* and—

(oh God!)

Pika Save.

Still, I checked the media store, and, to my surprise, images of Charizard and Venusaur greeted me on the home page. *Pokémon FireRed* and *LeafGreen*—the real ones, not odd counterfeits—waited for bored prisoners to pay and play.

Pokémania ensued. Half the dorm bought one version; some people even purchased both versions. I'd played the games' story many times: the original *Red* and *Blue* versions and *Pokémon Yellow*, the Gameboy Advance remakes (which were the versions available to us), and, most recently, on Nintendo Switch with *Pokémon Let's Go Eevee* and *Let's Go Pikachu*. I became known in the dorm as the *Pokémon* guru and helped others beat gym leaders, conquer the *Pokémon* League, and—of course—catch 'em all.

Though multiplayer functionality was disabled—they didn't want us communicating, I guess, even if all we could do was battle and trade—the addition of the games created a bond throughout the dorm. For a few dreamlike weeks, tension abated, and the dorm quieted while inmates stumbled around like *The Walking Dead*, their faces buried in screens. Envision *Pokémon Go*-level dissociation without the danger of walking off a cliff or stepping into traffic. All was well.

As I guided others through the games' difficult puzzles and pixelated terrains, people began to ask questions. *Did you buy* Pokémon *yet? When are you buying* Pokémon? My usual answer: when someone adds money to my media account. That was, at least in part, true.

Despite the syrupy, sweet nostalgia, *Pokémon* served as a stark reminder of life before prison.

Pokémon brought forth memories of my cousin Dante. As children, we were obsessed with *Pokémon*. When Ruby and Sapphire versions were released, I walked ten long little-kid minutes to his house to check out the new gameplay and scope out the new species of *Pokémon*. Excited to play and consumed with jealousy at the fact that his parents—one of them *my* uncle whom I technically knew longer because I was born first—bought him both versions when I had none, I stole one. It was only fair.

Hours later, after his parents called my grandma, I walked back, pretended to search—under beds where clouds of dust roamed free, under couches hiding food crumbs, and in the nooks of the pantry—eventually I placed the cartridge in a spot we had checked at least one hundred times, and acted shocked when I found it. "It must have just been hiding real hard," I said and shrugged.

Nearly two decades later, Dante and I played *Pokémon* together regularly, battling and trading whenever Nintendo released a new game, until my incarceration.

As I grew older, I wondered when I would actually grow up, start to truly feel my age. Sure, life threw more responsibility my way and despite never playing a sport that required catching things, I handled it well, considering. At my big-boy jobs, I've met people like me—adults in their late twenties/early thirties who played *Pokémon* in their free time. Take, for example, Sanchez: father of two beautiful little girls.

He humored me when I asked to play together, as in he kicked my ass handily in battles but slowly. Sanchez was ranked nationally in competitions and tournaments, and he created teams that complemented each other in battle. I played for fun, and knew I stood no chance, but sometimes winning really wasn't everything.

I never told him I was going to prison; I just disappeared. When I am released, however, I plan on dusting the cobwebs from the screen of my Nintendo Switch, firing it up and finally beating him in battle.

While in college, I worked at the Wendy's on campus. There I met Pito. When he sauntered to my register, my heart began pounding like some unsteady drum, and sweat pooled on my forehead until gravity dragged it down my face. Many times, I forced someone else to take his order because, as shift supervisor, I could.

Despite my awkwardness, we became friends. Throughout the decade that followed, our Poké-sessions migrated from the handheld Nintendo 3DS to the hybrid Switch, and survived Pito's move across the country. Though the consoles and our lives changed drastically, our Snapchats and story progress usually devolved into something more primal. With or without clothes, *Pokémon* connected two coasts and two lives as different as the vast landscapes—from arid desert to sprawling mountains—dividing them.

When I hit rock bottom, *Pokémon* provided me comfort like a familiar scent or favorite blanket or a hug from my grandma. In the eighteen months between my fatal crash and starting my sentence, I purposely allowed casual partying to become full-blown addiction. Depression and anxiety surrounding my future crashed around my head as waves ravaged boats in a storm. I knew I was going to prison—of that there was no doubt—so I simply stopped giving a fuck. I drank and sniffed coke all day, whether at home or at work. Properly wasted, personal hygiene to the wayside, and responsibilities neglected, the intricacies of the story and ever-improving graphics enveloped me and my squalor, transporting me temporarily to the world of *Pokémon*.

***

I write this now with my money-phagic tablet on the dayroom table next to me. *Pokémon* isn't downloaded. I couldn't force myself to buy it, though I've had ample opportunities. The initial hubbub has waned considerably, but sometimes I still see a few stragglers with their fingers wrapped passionately around nostalgia's neck, trying to catch the legendary *Pokémon*, Mewtwo. I smile.

My love for *Pokémon*, however, has not faltered. The decision to abstain from the reverie of play was one of personal protection. Seeing the joy *Pokémon* sparked in a miserable, dreary prison dorm brought me genuine happiness. Like a thunderbolt from a wild Pikachu, the craze electrified me, gave me hope that my future was not destined for everlasting gloom. Still, I couldn't give in to the desire to join the fray. For my own sake.

Pokémon reminded me of the good and bad times of innocence and of hardship. Best *and* worst of all, *Pokémon* reminded me of freedom. A new generation of *Pokémon* was released in November 2022. I know that when I get home, whenever that may be, adventure awaits.

ABOUT THE CONTRIBUTORS

- a.d. (she/her) is an emerging bisexual poet and visual artist. She is passionate about classical mythology, which serves as an inspiration for her work. She is currently working on her first poetry collection. You can also find her on Tumblr under the name *godstained*.

- Abhishek Udaykumar is a writer, filmmaker and painter from India. He graduated from Royal Holloway University of London with English and Creative Writing. His narratives reflect the human condition of rural and urban communities and explore eternal landscapes through film and prose. His writing has appeared in different literary journals and he has made thirteen independent films

- Abu Ibrahim (he/him), popularly known as IB, is a Nigerian poet whose work has had tremendous influence. Some of his works have also been published in literary outfits in Canada, the United States, the United Kingdom, and more. He reads for Fahmidan.

- Alexis David (she/her) is a poet who holds an MFA from New England College. Dancing Girl Press published her chapbook "The Names of Animals I Have Loved." Links to her other published work can be found here: https://alexisldavid.wixsite.com/alexis.

- Allison Whittenberg is an award-winning novelist and playwright. Her poetry has appeared in *Columbia Review, Feminist Studies, J Journal,* and *New Orleans Review*. Whittenberg is a six-time Pushcart Prize nominee. *Driving with a Poetic License and* and *They Were Horrible Cooks* are her collections of poetry.

- Annie Williams is a writer based in Fraser, Michigan that graduated from Oakland University with a Bachelors in Creative Writing. Her work has appeared in the publications of Fatal Flaw Literary Magazine, Sigma Tau Delta The Rectangle, Broken Antler Magazine, Nuestras Voces, Swallow The Moon, Echo Cognito, and Wingless Dreamer Publisher. She also has three poetry collections, her most recent one titled *Metal Poetry*. When she is not writing, she is either rocking out at a concert or staying at home watching a horror movie.

- Arani Acharjee is an emerging writer from Kolkata, India. She has beenpassionate about writing since her pre-teen days. She published her debut poetry book in 2021 and has co-authored ten anthologies till date.

- Audrey Zee Whitesides is a poet & musician living in Philadelphia, PA. Her work touches desire, affect, queerness, capital, & the social. You can find her with artists like Speedy Ortiz & Mal Blum or in the world as a hater.

- Aysha Siddiqui, (she/her) is a young Pakistani-American writer located near Seattle. She is inspired by her culture, nature, and the people around her in her writing.

- Carolina Mata (she/her) is a queer Xicana writer and bruja with an MFA from CSU, Fresno. Her work can be found in The San Joaquin Review, The Painted Cave, Wild Blue Zine, Psychopomp Magazine, & elsewhere. She's currently a Social Media Co-Director and Flash Reader at Split Lip Magazine.

- Cat Speranzini (she/her) is a New England based poet and novelist. Her debut full length poetry collection "Watercolor Souls" was released through Grey Coven Publishing in January 2024. Her work has also appeared in the Eunoia Review and FUCKUS magazine. Her short story "The Cactus" will be appearing in the next Querencia Press anthology. She writes poetry about the aftermath of heartbreak and trauma with a focus on introspection and shadow work. In her spare time Cat loves reading horror novels, horseback riding, and supporting local music. She is a mom of two toddlers, the honorary drum tech for the band No Detour, and an editor at Grey Coven Publishing.

- Christian Barragan (he/him) is a graduate from California State University Northridge. Raised in Riverside, CA, he aims to become a novelist or editor. He currently reads submissions for Flash Fiction Magazine. His work has appeared in the Raven Review, the Frogmore Papers, and Caustic Frolic, among others.

- Longlisted for the 2023 National Poetry Competition, Christian Ward's (he/him) poetry has recently appeared in Acumen, Dream Catcher, Free the Verse, Loch Raven Review, The Shore and The Westchester Review.

- Claire Winter (she/her) is a librarian, living in Kent, England. Her work has previously been published by The Wee Sparrow Press, Gypsophila Magazine, and in the anthology, Kaleidoscopic Minds. When not writing, she enjoys singing and crocheting.

- CLS Sandoval, PhD (she/her) is a writer and communication professor accomplished in film, academia, and creative writing who performs, writes, signs, and rarely relaxes. CLS is raising her daughter, son, and dog with her husband in Walnut, CA.

- Daniel is alive, and he dares you to prove otherwise. His work has appeared in over thirty publications, including 'Havik' and 'Ripples in Space.' He's got some books on Amazon. X: @Danny_Deisinger. Website: saturdaystory-Time.weebly.com.

- Daniel Schulz (he/him) is a U.S.-German writer known for the book and exhibition *Kathy Acker in Seattle*, various publications in literary and academic journals such as *Gender Forum, the Milton Review,* and *Fragmented Voices*. He has published two chapbooks *Welfare State* and *No Change to Abus*e. IG: @danielschulzpoet

- David M. Alper's forthcoming poetry collection is *Hush*. His work appears in *Variant Literature, Washington Square Review, Oxford Magazine*, and elsewhere. He is an educator in New York City.

- Devon Neal (he/him) is a Kentucky poet whose work has appeared in many publications, including HAD, Stanchion, Stone Circle Review, Livina Press, and was nominated for Best of the Net. He currently lives in Bardstown, KY with his wife and 3 children.

- Elena Sirett (they/them) is a queer, neurodivergent and mentally ill folk-punk musician, storyteller and writer. Their work is eclectic, honest and visceral.

- Eliza Scudder (she/her/hers) is a writer who creates comics and short stories inspired by her life. She writes about dreams, astrology, and childhood memories. You can follow her on Instagram @elizascudderwriting.

- Jack Anthony (he/they) is an emerging poet, writer and editor from Meanjin/Brisbane, Australia. His work has appeared in The Arboretum, Ink & Inclusion and Enbylife, among other publications.

- Jessi Carman (she/they) is a lifelong storyteller trying to find something that feels solid in the void. She writes poetry, prose, and nonfiction but is least protective of her poetry. They love books, film, crystals, their cats, and all strange things.

- Jordan Nishkian (she/her) is an Armenian-Portuguese writer based in California. Her prose and poetry explore themes of duality and have been featured in national and international publications.

- Justine Witkowski (any pronouns) is a queer writer and artist based out of the southwestern US. In their work, they are interested in exploring transience, rebirth and abjection. They are in their fourth year of conjunctive art and anthropology degrees.

- Kashawn Taylor (he/him) is a poet and essayist based in CT. His poetry, fiction, and essays have been published by Prison Journalism Project, the Indiana Review, the Blotter Magazine, and more.

- Meet Kerith Collins, the wordsmith who brews her verses with a dash of caffeine and weaves tapestries of shimmering verse. When she's not scribbling sonnets, you'll find her daydreaming about sipping lattes and poetry flowing like rivers of espresso.

- Kevin B is a writer and poet from New England. They have been published in Esoterica, Havik, New Plains Review, and Auvert Magazine. They are the George Lila Award winner for Short Fiction, and the Barely Seen Featured Poet of 2023.

- Lana Valdez is a Florida-raised poetess and sometimes filmmaker living in Southern California. Her work has been published in Dream Boy Book Club, Spectra, Expat, Higj Horse and others, and her short films are on her YouTube channel.

- Born in Germany, Lara Konrad spent her adolescing years in Mexico and lived close to a decade in New York where she received her BA in Creative Writing at *The New School*. Since her MFA at *Sandberg Institute* (Amsterdam, Holland), she has written for a plethora of literary and cultural publications, as well as art institutions. Some favorite publishing platforms include: NYTyrant, Civilization, Worms, Wonder, Die Zeit, Literarische WELT, Das Magazin. In 2020, a second (revised) edition of her poetry collection *Mother, We All Have Been Lonely and Lovely* was published with Gato Negro Ediciones. Her first novel appears in spring 2025. She is currently at work on a new book about the middle. Since the outbreak of the pandemic, she has been based in Munich, Germany.

- Liam Strong (they/them) is a queer neurodivergent writer from Michigan. They are the author of the chapbook *Everyone's Left the Hometown Show* (Bottlecap Press, 2023). Find them on Instagram/Twitter: @beanbie666
- Liz Bajjalieh (She/they/he) is a disabled queer diasporic Palestinian and Irish poet and visual artist living on Ojibwe Land. Their poetry focuses on the nexus of healing, spirituality, and liberation for all. Her written work has been featured in the Friend's Journal, Waging Nonviolence, Handbasket Zine, and previously in Querencia Press. They will be publishing their first book SCREAM Until You Know What God Is with Fernwood Press later this year. His art can be found at @dandelion.tea.art on Instagram.
- Maeva Wunn is a bisexual, non-binary, and neurodivergent writer of poetry and prose, crafter, history buff, and music enthusiast living with chronic illnesses. They currently reside in Iowa with their spouse and cats.
- Marcella Cavallo (she/her) is a German poet with Italian roots. For her, inspiration is found everywhere, as long as you keep your eyes and heart open. Her work appeared in the anthology "Songs of Revolution" published by Sunday Mornings at the River.
- Mark Kangas (he/him), born on June 16, 1997, lives in Calumet, Michigan. He's relatively aimless in his career choices (carpenter, draftsman, now custodian) but persistent in his pursuit of growth in music, visual art, and poetry.
- Michaela (she/her) is a 26 year old woman living in Philly. Michaela pulls inspiration from her experience as a queer woman working in hospitality & love of connection. She has not practiced proper grammar in 6 years but has a lot of feelings.
- nat raum (they/them) is a disabled artist, writer, and genderless disaster based in Baltimore. They're the editor-in-chief of fifth wheel press and the author of you stupid slut, the abyss is staring back, and others. Find them online at natraum.com.
- Nico Vickers is a poet, teacher, and aspiring novelist with a deep passion for languages, mythology, folklore, and religion. Fluent in Croatian and English, she draws inspiration from the intersections of cultures and the power of storytelling.
- Nikoletta Nousiopoulos is a poet, writer and educator who resides in Southeastern Connecticut. She has published poetry in various journals including: The Fairy Tale Review, Tammy, ethel, Whiskey Island, poineertown, Thin Noon and Peach Mag.
- Rachel Chitofu is a poet and third-year medical student from Harare, Zimbabwe. She won South Africa's New Coin poetry prize in 2021.
- Rebecca (Becks) Carlyle is based in Santa Cruz, CA. She spends her time exploring the outdoors with her dog, Scout. Her work is fueled by copious amounts of coffee. In 2020, she published her first novel, "Finding Alice."
- Robert Castagna (he/him/his) teaches Pictures and Poetry at his local senior center. A photographer and poet, he has received the Massachusetts Cultural Council Photography Fellowship and The Artist's Resource Trust Grant.

- Sam Woods is a full time janitor, perpetual student, lifelong writer and avid reader. Her work has been featured in Willawaw Journal and Wunderlit with future publications coming this spring.
- Sebastian Vice (He/Him) is a functioning degenerate who, between bouts of crippling nihilism, manages to co-run Outcast Press and Translucent Eyes Press. He sometimes pens poems, short stories, and novellas. Find him on Twitter at: @sebastian_vice.
- Toshiya Kamei (they/them) takes inspiration from fairy tales, folklore, and mythology. They attempt to reimagine the past, present, and future while shifting between various perspectives and points of view.
- Yuyi Chen (they/them) is a poet, fiction writer, and hopefully-would-be scholar from Sichuan, China. They are now in a PhD program in anthropology at Johns Hopkins University. Writing literary work in English is a newly found delight for them.
- Zaira Gomez is an emerging writer from Pennsylvania currently located in Mexico City. As a queer Mexican Femme, her works explore themes of adolescence, femininity, sexuality, and post trauma healing. Her work is published or forthcoming in The Sonora Review, Entre Magazine and she was awarded a seat at the Juniper Summer Institute Retreat. She is working on her first chapbook entitled, Sentidos de Mi Mismo.

OTHER TITLES FROM QUERENCIA

Allison by Marisa Silva-Dunbar

GIRL. by Robin Williams

Retail Park by Samuel Millar

Every Poem a Potion, Every Song a Spell by Stephanie Parent

songs of the blood by Kate MacAlister

Love Me Louder by Tyler Hurula

God is a Woman by TJ McGowan

Learning to Float by Alyson Tait

Fever by Shilo Niziolek

Cutting Apples by Jomé Rain

Girl Bred from the 90s by Olivia Delgado

Wax by Padraig Hogan

When Memory Fades by Faye Alexandra Rose

The Wild Parrots of Marigny by Diane Elayne Dees

Hospital Issued Writing Notebook by Dan Flore III

Knees in the Garden by Christina D Rodriguez

Provocative is a Girl's Name by Mimi Flood

Bad Omens by Jessica Drake-Thomas

Beneath the Light by Laura Lewis-Waters

Ghost Hometowns by Giada Nizzoli

Dreamsoak by Will Russo

the abyss is staring back by nat raum

How Long Your Roots Have Grown by Sophia-Maria Nicolopoulos

The World Eats Butterflies Like You by Isabelle Quilty

Playing Time in Tongues by Vita Lerman

unloving the knife by Lilith Kerr

5 Spirits in My Mouth by Pan Morigan

You Shouldn't Worry About the Frogs by Eliza Marley

Now Let's Get Brunch: A Collection of RuPaul's Drag Race Twitter Poetry by Alex Carrigan

The Dissection of a Tiger by Tyler Walter

Reasons Why We're Angry by Sophia Isabella Murray

An Absurd Palate by Alysa Levi-D'Ancona

Stained: an anthology of writing about menstruation Curated by Rachel Neve-Midbar & Jennifer Saunders
Tender is the Body by Alise Versella
House of Filth by Kei Vough Korede
The Beginning of Leaving by Elsa Valmidiano
TASEREDGED (watch out!) by Tommy Wyatt
Dear Nora, by c. michael kinsella
adulteress by Chloe Hanks
Sessions of a Sandstorm by Isaac Miebi Mendez
atrophy by Shilo Niziolek
twenty-twenty-twenty-twenty-one by Leah Soeiro
Hymns from the Sisters – Emma Conally-Barklem
Buffy's House of Mirrors by Kim Malinowski & Gabby Gilliam
Little Lenny Gets His Horns by Remi Recchia & Victoria Garcia-Boswell
Domestic Bodies by Jennifer Ruth Jackson
The Edge of Hope by Robin Williams
Survivalism for Hedonists by Dylan McNulty-Holmes
What Hauts Me the Most by Chimen Georgette Kouri
Proof of the Sun by Eve Ott
The Magpie Funeral by Adam J. Galanski-De León
vermilion by Samantha Erron Gibbon
The Un-Inquired by Renee Chen
Vanishing Below the Waist by Ellie White
Here in Sanctuary—Whirling by D. Dina Friedman
Mexican Bird by Luis Lopez-Maldonado
Diary of Rhymes by Jemelia Moseley
A Peculiar Day in the Douro Valley by Benjamin Eric
sun eater by dre levant
Pigeon House by Shilo Niziolek
Of Lost Things by Dani De Luca
Misplaced Organs & Various Saints by Dante Émile
RECURRENT by Darla Mottram
GUNK by Noah David Roberts
DreamRot {Forsaken} by Ami J. Sanghvi

Printed in the USA
CPSIA information can be obtained
at www.ICGtesting.com
LVHW012030300824
789746LV00043B/318